Praise for
Delicious and Suspicious

"Sassy." —*Publishers Weekly*

"An entertaining read . . . Just like the pork barbeque and spicy corn muffins that fill the bellies of the fictitious patrons of Aunt Pat's, the Southern flavor is what makes this novel unique. The characters live and breathe on the page, not as stereotypes of Southerners but as colorful personalities that complement the Memphis setting." —*Romance Novel News*

"This entertaining regional amateur sleuth gives the audience a taste of living in [Memphis], especially owning a restaurant in a tourist-attraction city . . . With a strong, fully seasoned support cast who enhance the whodunit, *Delicious and Suspicious* is truly scrumptious." —*Genre Go Round Reviews*

"A saucy Southern mystery!"
—Krista Davis, national bestselling author of
The Diva Cooks a Goose

"Don't let that folksy facade fool you. Lulu Taylor is one intrepid amateur sleuth."
—Laura Childs, *New York Times* bestselling author of
Scones & Bones

"Lulu Taylor serves up the best barbeque in Memphis. Never been to her restaurant, Aunt Pat's? Well then, pick up a copy of Riley Adams's enjoyable *Delicious and Suspicious*, slide into a booth, and follow Lulu as she tracks down a killer with the help of her wacky friends and family. You'll feel transported to Beale Street. Oh, and did I mention the mouthwatering recipes at the end?"
—Julie Hyzy, author of *Buffalo West Wing*

"Riley Adams's first book, *Delicious and Suspicious*, adds a dash of Southern humor to a sauté of murder and mayhem that is as good as cold banana pudding on a hot summer day. Lulu Taylor is a hoot! I look forward to reading the next book in the Memphis barbeque series!" —Joyce Lavene, coauthor of *A Touch of Gold*

Berkley Prime Crime titles by Riley Adams

DELICIOUS AND SUSPICIOUS
FINGER LICKIN' DEAD

FINGER LICKIN'
DEAD

Riley Adams

BERKLEY PRIME CRIME, NEW YORK

THE BERKLEY PUBLISHING GROUP
Published by the Penguin Group
Penguin Group (USA) Inc.
375 Hudson Street, New York, New York 10014, USA
Penguin Group (Canada), 90 Eglinton Avenue East, Suite 700, Toronto, Ontario M4P 2Y3, Canada
(a division of Pearson Penguin Canada Inc.)
Penguin Books Ltd., 80 Strand, London WC2R 0RL, England
Penguin Group Ireland, 25 St. Stephen's Green, Dublin 2, Ireland (a division of Penguin Books Ltd.)
Penguin Group (Australia), 250 Camberwell Road, Camberwell, Victoria 3124, Australia
(a division of Pearson Australia Group Pty. Ltd.)
Penguin Books India Pvt. Ltd., 11 Community Centre, Panchsheel Park, New Delhi–110 017, India
Penguin Group (NZ), 67 Apollo Drive, Rosedale, North Shore 0632, New Zealand
(a division of Pearson New Zealand Ltd.)
Penguin Books (South Africa) (Pty.) Ltd., 24 Sturdee Avenue, Rosebank, Johannesburg 2196,
South Africa

Penguin Books Ltd., Registered Offices: 80 Strand, London WC2R 0RL, England

This is a work of fiction. Names, characters, places, and incidents either are the product of the author's imagination or are used fictitiously, and any resemblance to actual persons, living or dead, business establishments, events, or locales is entirely coincidental. The publisher does not have any control over and does not assume any responsibility for author or third-party websites or their content.

PUBLISHER'S NOTE: The recipes contained in this book are to be followed exactly as written. The publisher is not responsible for your specific health or allergy needs that may require medical supervision. The publisher is not responsible for any adverse reactions to the recipes contained in this book.

FINGER LICKIN' DEAD

A Berkley Prime Crime Book / published by arrangement with the author

PRINTING HISTORY
Berkley Prime Crime mass-market edition / June 2011

Copyright © 2011 by Penguin Group (USA) Inc.
Cover design by Annette Fiore DeFex.
Cover illustration by Hugh Syme.
Interior text design by Laura K. Corless.

ISBN: 978-0-425-24191-2

BERKLEY® PRIME CRIME
Berkley Prime Crime Books are published by The Berkley Publishing Group,
a division of Penguin Group (USA) Inc.,
375 Hudson Street, New York, New York 10014.
BERKLEY® PRIME CRIME and the PRIME CRIME logo are trademarks of Penguin Group (USA) Inc.

PRINTED IN THE UNITED STATES OF AMERICA

10 9 8 7 6 5 4 3 2 1

To my family

Acknowledgments

My thanks to my editor, Emily Beth Rapoport, for her invaluable help and encouragement.

To my agent, Ellen Pepus, for her solid advice and support.

Hart Johnson for her helpful suggestions.

To Ann and John Haire, my friends in Memphis.

To the staff at Graceland for their help with my research.

Special thanks to my mother, Beth Spann, for being a fantastic and enthusiastic first reader.

To my extended family for all their support.

To the online writing community for the inspiration and advice it provides me.

And thanks so much to my husband, Coleman, and my children, Riley and Elizabeth Ruth, for their constant love and encouragement.

Chapter 1

"Somebody," said Cherry darkly, "should kill that guy."

"Only as a last resort," said her good friend Peggy Sue. "Have we exhausted all the other possibilities? Rolled his house with toilet paper? Made prank phone calls? Shaken pepper in his sweet tea?" She gave a lilting laugh.

"I'm not so clear what his punishable offense is," said Lulu, tilting her head to one side as she pondered and endangering the small bun of white hair at the top of her head. "We don't like Adam Cawthorn because he's dating Evelyn? Because he's too good-looking?"

"Because he's snarky," growled Cherry. "Besides, I think he's taking advantage of Evelyn, who is, as y'all know, one of my favorite people in the world. He's always asking for a little bit of money here and a little bit there. Besides, he has a weak chin. What good is it if you've got looks but a weak chin?"

Lulu considered this. "Still, it doesn't sound too awful, Cherry. Evelyn's loaded with money—maybe it doesn't bother her to share it a little bit. Does he treat her badly?"

"He doesn't treat her *well*," said Flo thoughtfully.

"On the upside," said Lulu, "he sure does eat some barbeque. He's good for business." Lulu was the owner of Memphis's famous Aunt Pat's Barbeque, right there on Beale Street. As a second-generation owner, she knew by now what made for a good customer. And Adam Cawthorn, despite his shortcomings, had one of the biggest components of a good customer—frequent visits.

"No, *he's* not good for business," said Cherry. "*Evelyn* is. She's the one shelling out the money for him to eat here. And think about it—he's separated from his wife. He's been running around on *her*, so why wouldn't he be doing the same with Evelyn? Besides, she's already been married to him once before. Clearly that didn't work out so well, so why try for mistake number two?"

"Heads up, y'all—Evelyn's coming over," hissed Jeanne, looking across the restaurant's crowded dining room.

Lulu thought for the hundredth time how lucky she was to have such a great group of regulars at her restaurant. These ladies, who were some of her favorite guests at Aunt Pat's Barbeque, were dubbed the Graces by everyone because they were docents at Graceland. They were colorful, fun—and loyal, thought Lulu as she watched them struggle to be supportive of Evelyn.

The Graces and Lulu looked like butter wouldn't melt in their mouth by the time Evelyn got up to their booth. But Evelyn wouldn't have noticed if they'd all been wagging their tongues about her right when she walked up. She was sitting high up on cloud nine. Lulu frequently reflected that it was a good thing Evelyn was so nice; she wouldn't have been tolerable otherwise, with her good looks, good luck, and boatload of money. Most of the Graces were happy members of the Fabulous Fifties club, but Evelyn hadn't quite joined yet. Peggy Sue was already part of the Sassy Sixties—which Lulu had belonged to for quite a while.

Evelyn plopped down in the wooden booth right next to Lulu and impulsively gave her a hug and a smile that lit up the room. "I am *so* glad to see y'all! Isn't it a gorgeous day?"

No, thought Lulu. Actually, it was a pretty miserable day outside, unless you were partial to torrential rain. But she smiled and nodded.

Evelyn realized her error and gave an out-of-character giggle. "Whoops! My bad—it's pouring, isn't it? Well, we do need the rain. Sometimes that's the best kind of weather to get—one with lots of rain in it."

"Where," asked Flo in a dry voice, "is Adam?"

"Nearby, of course. I want to keep him as close as possible. He'll be over in a minute—he just popped into the men's room. Can you believe I had him all to myself—that I was *married* to him—and then let him go? I must have been nuts."

And this, thought Lulu, is how history rewrites itself.

Cherry, though, seemed less interested in the sunshine and roses version of the story. "Wasn't Adam the husband who splashed his money all over Memphis? Who said ugly things about you behind your back to his friends? Who tried to make you feel lower than a lizard's belly?" She tapped her glass of sweet tea against the red and white checkered tablecloth with every point.

Evelyn frowned as if considering these allegations carefully. "I don't believe Adam *is* that husband, Cherry, no. I believe you've gotten him mixed up with another husband."

Being Southern ladies, no one mentioned Evelyn's excessive number of ex-husbands. It wouldn't be seemly. Evelyn, though, felt free to mention that fact herself with no compunction.

"And here comes trouble now," said Cherry. But she said it enough under her breath that only Lulu could hear it. Lulu winked at her.

Adam Cawthorn was a nice-looking man, thought Lulu. If you were to describe him to somebody, you would use only the finest adjectives—broad shoulders; thick, blond hair; perfect teeth. But there was something that definitely didn't ring true with Adam. That perfect smile was just a little bit spiteful. Maybe that was it.

He certainly seemed pleasant enough today, though. He walked over to the booth and greeted Lulu and the

Graces. "Honey, did you order me up some red beans and rice?" he asked Evelyn.

She nodded eagerly. "I sure did. It should be coming soon." She turned to Lulu and said, "Adam just loves those red beans and rice." Her eyes shone like a teenager in puppy love. "And he's a real food expert. Did you know that he used to own a restaurant?"

There was a groan from Cherry that wasn't even all that muted. Evelyn had mentioned that little fact to them quite a few times, thought Lulu. "I think it's wonderful," said Lulu. "To think he likes our red beans and rice so much!"

Cherry said innocently enough, but in a tone that Lulu knew meant trouble, "And how does Adam stand on Elvis? Is he as big a fan of the King as we all are?" She blinked her big green eyes.

Adam made a face. "I don't see how on earth y'all spend so much time at Graceland every week."

"It's the highlight of our week," said plump Peggy Sue with surprise. "The very pinnacle of it! We just love the staff—they're practically family to us. And every time I go out there, I discover something interesting and different that I hadn't seen before."

"And they *depend* on us at Graceland," said Jeanne earnestly. "The fans that come through are sometimes so thrilled to be there that it's easy for them to forget themselves and start climbing over the velvet ropes to try to visit with the King for a spell. We help keep them straight."

The trays of barbeque ribs and sides of beans and

spicy cornbread arrived at the table. Adam took a big mouthful of ribs, which he ate noisily. "Delicious!" he proclaimed, smacking his lips. Cherry was long past hiding anything and looked disgusted with his table manners.

"Darling," he said, reaching out and squeezing Evelyn's hand. "I've got a wonderful idea. Let's go out tonight and really have a night on the town. We'll have a Beale Street night. Work our way down the street, eating soul food, listening to music, and drinking beer. We can even watch the street flippers backflip down Beale. What do you think?" There was a little whiny tinge to his voice that grated on Lulu's nerves.

"You have the best ideas!" said Evelyn. She beamed at him. "Want to shoot for eight o'clock?"

Cherry cleared her throat and deliberately ignored Adam. "Tonight's Bunko night. Remember? It's over at Bertha's house. And I believe you promised to bring your famous Crock-Pot spinach dip. With the artichokes in it." Cherry turned to Lulu. "Have you ever had it? It's to die for. All that cheese just bubbling off your cracker—it's a meal all by itself."

"Bunko!" Evelyn slapped her palm on the table with enough force to make nervous Jeanne jump. "I *knew* I was forgetting something. Shoot!"

Adam's mouth curled downward. "Can't you just give the cards a pass tonight? We'd already made plans."

"It's dice. Not cards. And it's been a plan for months," said Cherry through gritted teeth.

"Sugar, I just can't give it a pass tonight," said Evelyn.

"Last month I didn't make it because I had that nasty cold that knocked me out. I wouldn't have been able to go without toting a supersized box of tissue with me and my own wastebasket. Then, the month before *that* I couldn't go because it was my mama's birthday and Mama wanted me to come by and do what we always do for her birthday."

"What do you always do for your mama's birthday?" asked Peggy Sue in a curious voice.

"We go to the cafeteria. It's all Mama wants to do. She does love her fried okra, dinner rolls, and meat loaf. We walk through the cafeteria line with our trays and Mama practically claps her hands in excitement over all the choices."

"Ahh," nodded Flo. Evelyn's mama was in her nineties. Ladies in their nineties were allowed any number of eccentricities. "The food in there is awfully salty, though, isn't it?"

"It's salty to me, but not to Mama. She brings her own bottle of soy sauce in her pocketbook and pours it all over the rice. Says she likes international flavors. And you know, the salt hasn't killed her yet, has it? She's ninety-five years old, playing bridge every day, going to that 'sit-er-cize' class at the retirement home twice a week. . . . She's got to be doing something right. Between the Jack Daniels, soy sauce, and peppermints, *something* is working out for her."

Adam's restlessness had progressed to the point where he looked to be about to jump out of his skin. "Fine. Just fine. I guess you can find time to squeeze me in later in the week? I know your schedule in your appointment book is really tight with all your activities."

Cherry rolled her eyes at Lulu. Lulu had to admit that he did sound pitiful. But luckily she saw someone coming into the Aunt Pat's dining room that they could visit with a while and shift the focus off Adam.

Adam apparently caught Cherry's eye roll because he shifted his displeasure to her. He looked at her thoughtfully, taking in her bright, tight clothing and clunky bracelets. His gaze rested on Cherry's Elvis helmet. He said, "You do realize you're wearing your motorcycle helmet, don't you?"

Cherry bristled. No one but a newcomer would even notice that Cherry had *on* a helmet, thought Lulu. It had Elvis on the side and Cherry wore it almost everywhere. She claimed that life was too dangerous to face without a helmet.

"Of course I know that. I happen to ascribe to the belief that I'll live a much longer life this way. With this helmet, Elvis is acting as my guardian angel. If I'm in a car accident? I'll have my helmet protecting me. Get thrown off my riding mower? Luckily, I'll be wearing a helmet. Tornado pops up? I'm protected from debris."

Adam snorted. "And what dangers are you facing here in the bosom of your friends in the middle of a barbeque restaurant?"

"Bad company," said Cherry. "Only my helmet doesn't help too much with that."

"Oh, look, y'all—here comes Tudy," said Lulu, interjecting before the situation got too heated. Adam didn't know what Cherry could be like when she got all fired up. "Let's try to cheer her up—she's had such a rough couple of months."

All the ladies' faces immediately registered an appropriate level of sympathy and concern. Adam's brows raised curiously as a brightly dressed, well-preserved middle-aged woman with lots of large pieces of jewelry approached.

"Come sit with us, Tudy," urged Evelyn. "How are things going for you?"

"Awful!" said Tudy, although she still had a broad grin on her face. "Hi, girls!" she said brightly and hugged as many of the Graces as she could reach. "Could I get a barbeque plate with cornbread?" she asked the hovering waitress.

Lulu said, "Tudy, Ben fried up some okra today, too, in case you want any of that."

Tudy said, "You *bet* I want some fried okra!" The waitress added it to the order and hurried away. "I don't know what Ben puts in that breading, but that okra is the best I've ever put in my mouth. I wish he'd add it to the main menu instead of just having it as a special sometimes."

Tudy pulled up a chair to the end of the booth. "Where was I?" she asked. "Oh, I remember. Awful! It's been terrible, ladies . . . and gentleman," she said, with a nod at Adam. "You know that restaurant was my *life* for so many years. And Oliver's, too. I've been at Aunt Pat's every day this week because I've got to be in *somebody's* restaurant. Besides, this place has been part

of my life for so long that it feels like home to me. My
mama used to come here," Tudy said to Adam. "And you
look around and you feel like you're a special guest . . .
all the pictures and college pennants and baseballs and
memorabilia on the wall where you can hardly even see
the bricks!"

Evelyn explained to Adam. "Tudy's husband owned a
restaurant for years."

"A wonderful restaurant. And it always did really
well," said Lulu stoutly. "We'd eat there anytime we
weren't over at Aunt Pat's. Good food that stuck to your
ribs."

"Rib-stickiness being a good trait for a meal," murmured Adam in a voice that *could* be translated as
sarcasm.

Tudy beamed at Lulu. "Aren't you the sweetest!"
Then she said to Adam, "Then Oliver had this nasty review in the paper. That restaurant reviewer who has the
following like a rock star? Eppie Currian. She's on the
Twitter. She's on the Facebook. She's everywhere! And
people take her advice like it's gospel. They're just that
taken in by her."

Adam leaned a little closer to Tudy. "So what happened after that review?"

"You wouldn't *think* that one bad review would close
down a restaurant. That's *crazy*, right? After you've got
a group of regulars built up and a nice reputation and
been around for years and years? But that's just how de-
vout those followers of this Eppie Currian woman are.
They're gaga over her." Tudy looked bemused.

"Who is she again?" asked Adam.

The whole table frowned at him like they thought he was soft in the head. "He doesn't subscribe to the newspaper. He's just too busy to sit down for long enough to read it. Isn't that right, Adam?" said Evelyn protectively.

"Her name is Eppie Currian. Isn't that just the most revolting name? The paper was making a cutesy thing out of 'epicurean' for her pen name. She's incognito so she can visit the restaurants and be anonymous and then print hateful things. Anyway, it doesn't matter who she is. What matters is that she ruined us. And if it happened to us, it could happen to anybody." She gave Lulu a tired look.

"What's Oliver doing now?" asked Jeanne in a quiet voice.

"Driving me half out of my skull with annoyance is what Oliver's doing," said Tudy with a snort. "He's messing up my daily routine big-time. This morning? I came downstairs at my normal getting-up time and Oliver was on *my* laptop. Mine! And I always check my e-mails the very first thing in the morning because the girls like to e-mail me late at night after I've turned in." Tudy and Oliver had grown daughters who lived somewhere along the East Coast, as far as Lulu could remember.

Cherry winced. "That's hard. I like to check my e-mails first thing, too."

"And then? He finally hands me the laptop back. I get on it, and I *do* have a nice long e-mail from our older daughter, Janet. But do I get to read it? No. Because Oliver has picked up the morning newspaper and starts reading the stories to me. Reading them to me! Directly from the paper as if I don't know how to read for myself." Her face flushed from just the thought of it.

Lulu's daughter in law, Sara, had joined the group and listened in for a few minutes. She made a face. "It sounds like he has Retired Husband Syndrome," said Sara.

"Get out!" said Cherry. "There's no such thing."

"No, there is! And RHS has become a problem for millions of women worldwide," said Sara, bobbing her red head emphatically. "There was this article I read about it. Here these women are. . . . They've been queen of the castle for thirty or forty years. They've run their houses like generals—cleaning, cooking, running errands, making decisions. Then their husbands come home and they're bored and they start meddling in the household affairs. Why not try *this* brand of peanut butter? Did their wives know that they could make their own cleaner instead of buying it? Although I don't really see myself having that problem with Ben when he retires."

"You don't?" said Lulu. "I'd think he'd be itching to do something to keep busy if he didn't have the restaurant. He's always got to be moving around, doing something."

"He'd be off in the woods all day . . . subduing nature," said Sara. "I probably wouldn't see hide nor hair of him."

Evelyn looked adoringly at Adam, who looked coolly back at her. "Adam is so outgoing that I wouldn't see anything of him, either. He'd be dining out with friends or playing tennis or going to see a play or concert."

"I wish I could say the same about Oliver," said Tudy in a sad voice. "He doesn't golf, he doesn't hunt. He doesn't play bridge. He needs another job. Quick. Before he drives me crazy!"

Peggy Sue said, "When my husband retired, it was the shortest retirement in the world—it ended up being for only five days. The next thing he knew, he had a job at the meat counter at the Piggly Wiggly." She archly raised her eyebrows. "He criticized my dusting abilities. 'Missed a spot!' "

The Graces groaned and nodded.

Lulu said, "Can't Oliver find another restaurant job? Even if it's not *his* restaurant, it's still what he knows."

Tudy tapped her manicured nails on the table. "It's not as easy as you'd think. College students are competing for those positions now. And he's got his pride, too. He's been running a restaurant for so long that he doesn't want to do those little piddly jobs anymore. He needs to get rid of that pride, though—otherwise it's going to be all he has left."

"You know," said Lulu in a low voice, as if diners might hear her and run out the door, "we had one of those reviews in the morning paper today. From that Eppie Currian."

Chapter

2

Tudy sat back in the booth in alarm. "A bad one?"

"Awful."

"In that snarky, looking-down-her-nose tone?"

"As snarky as you can imagine," said Lulu.

"So how," asked Jeanne in a hushed voice, "is Ben doing? After reading that review and all? I know how proud Ben is of his cooking abilities and everybody *knows* he's the finest barbeque cook in all of Memphis. That review was pretty rough. I wasn't going to mention it, but since you brought it up . . ." The Graces all murmured a concerned echo.

"I suppose he's doing all right," said Lulu with a sigh as she thought about her son. "He's back there cooking, after all. Thank the Lord. It's just not the same when Ben's not wielding the spatula."

Sara said, "Ben was just *devastated* this morning

when he read that review. I won't be surprised if he ends up going home sick. He was that ill over it. He puts everything he has into his cooking and having somebody make fun of it was so hurtful to him. He's in desperate need of a hunting or fishing trip. It makes him so mad when he's put everything he's got into cooking and someone writes something so ugly about it."

"That reviewer is such a . . . such a smarty pants," fumed Jeanne. Lulu was fairly certain that a more derogatory name had been on the tip of Jeanne's tongue, but she was too much of a lady to use it. "What got me most of all is that she said Aunt Pat's 'wasn't Memphis enough.'"

Peggy Sue gasped. "But everybody knows this is *the* place in Memphis for barbeque ribs. Not *Memphis* enough? When the King himself came to this restaurant, played out on the porch, and left Aunt Pat a signed guitar? And the guitar is hanging right up on the wall over there? Is this food writer off her trolley?"

Lulu beamed at Peggy Sue. "You're sweet. But you know, it is her job. Whoever this Eppie Currian restaurant critic is."

"That's very nice of you to say so, Lulu," said Cherry, still fired up, "but the fact of the matter is that this person doesn't have to be snide and unpleasant. If she didn't like the food, she could just point out the problems in a professional way. Instead, she makes it personal and cutting."

"It wasn't *that* bad of a review," said Evelyn in a soothing voice.

"It was pretty bad," demurred Adam.

Cherry shot him a flaming look. "I thought you were too busy to subscribe to the paper!"

"He was reading my copy of the paper this morning, Cherry," said Evelyn. "He came over for an early morning coffee."

"Right," said Cherry through gritted teeth.

"'Aunt Pat's needs to be skewered.'" Sara quoted from the review. "That was the headline for the write-up."

"Y'all have been around for generations, though," said Tudy. "I just don't see the review hurting you like it hurt us."

"But *you'd* been around for years yourself. It wasn't like you were the new restaurant on the block or anything. Whether we like it or not, this girl has a lot of power and influence," said Lulu with a sigh. "Although I still say that the reason the food is so good here and that people keep coming back for more is that Aunt Pat's love of food is in every bite of her recipes."

"Makes me long for the days when Holden Parsons wrote up the reviews," said Tudy with a sigh. "He didn't sugarcoat his reviews, but he was *fair*. He could be tough on a place, but he wasn't going to be snide. And restaurants didn't end up closing their doors because of him."

"Where has Holden been lately? Usually he's in here every week, stuffing himself with some ribs. But I haven't seen him so far this week," said Lulu.

"This girl! Eppie. *She* happened to him. As soon as

she sashayed into the paper, his rear was kicked out onto the street. There's just no loyalty anymore, you know? He's a good friend of ours, and Oliver and I just hated seeing what happened to him. He used to be a regular at the restaurant. And now I see him just wandering around, looking lost. Wearing his bow tie. So sad."

"If this Eppie is anonymous, how do you know she was sashaying anywhere?" asked Adam dryly.

"Oh, believe me, honey, I know all about that kind of girl," said Tudy, shaking her head. "I don't have to *see* her to know everything about her. You can just tell it through the tone of what she's writing. Sassy! Thinks she knows everything. Smarty pants!"

"But food reporters are supposed to be anonymous," said Adam, looking bored. "That way the restaurant they're visiting won't make them a super-delicious meal and give them the best service. Right? They're supposed to get an accurate picture of what the restaurant is really like."

Lulu nodded. "That's right. But this Eppie seems like she's not all that concerned about the truth—she just wants to write funny copy. But Holden was sort of a well-known secret in the business. We weren't *supposed* to know who he was, but we did. He treated everyone fairly. If Holden wasn't happy about something, he also made sure to still say some good things about the restaurant, about the décor or something, even if the food was rotten."

Adam carefully put his plate aside, scooted off the

booth, and stood up. Evelyn stood up, too, smoothing down her expensive slacks. "I'll walk you to the door, sugar."

He did walk over to the door—but first he quickly walked up to the brick wall and compulsively straightened a picture of an Aunt Pat's regular holding up a huge fish and beaming.

"Now watch," said Cherry. "He's going to lean over, act sweet, then say something to her, and next thing you know, her hand is going to be dipping in her pocketbook and pulling out some twenties."

Flo squinted toward the door. Sure enough, Evelyn pressed some money real quick into Adam's hand before he walked out the door. "Whatta man," said Cherry in disgust.

"Maybe he's going to run some errands for her," said Jeanne.

"You are so good, Jeanne," said Flo. "Always looking for somebody's good side."

"Well you're not going to find it with Adam," said Cherry. "I think you could look for his good side with a microscope and not be able to find it."

"Not be able to find what?" asked Lulu's son, Ben. He was finally taking a break from the kitchen. He pulled up a chair near the booth and sat down next to Sara with a relieved sigh. Standing up for hours on end used to be easier than it was now that he was in his late forties.

"Evelyn's new old beau," said Sara.

"*That* joker? I hope she gets rid of him soon. There's something that's not right about that guy. He had Big

Jack cornered here a couple of days ago, and after he was done talking to him, Big Jack looked all pale and shaky."

"Big Jack? Big Jack Bratcher, the politician?" asked Flo. Ben nodded and Flo said, "Wonder what he told him to have him that shaken up? Every time I see Big Jack, he's got a beer in one hand, a puffy red face, and is bellowing out a laugh about something. Maybe he had the flu or strep throat when you saw him that day."

"Maybe. But he sure looked the picture of health up until Adam started talking to him," said Ben.

He looked over at the group of men who'd just come in the door. Big Ben, Buddy, and Morty were retired blues musicians, now in their eighties, who called Aunt Pat's their hangout. Sometimes they even played if there was a break in the band lineup in the evenings.

"Hey there," Ben called out to them.

Buddy and Morty looked over, but Big Ben was deaf as a post. Morty tapped his arm and he greeted Ben.

Buddy said, "Y'all sure looked awfully serious when we were walking in. Something going on?"

Ben said, "No, we were just fussing. We're not crazy about Evelyn's boyfriend, that's all."

"Know what I don't like about him?" said Morty. "He doesn't have a nickname. Nobody thinks highly enough of him to call him Bubba or Bud or Ace."

"Men who don't have nicknames bother me, too," said Ben, smoothing his mustache. "Maybe that's part of it."

"He should be Gator or something," bellowed Big

Ben. "This Adam nonsense—he just wants everybody to take him seriously."

"And he's too pretty," said Lulu, squinting thoughtfully. "He needs a rugged scar or something. If you put a wig on him, he'd pass as a girl."

"*I'll* give him a scar," said Cherry darkly.

"You are just dead set against the poor man," said Peggy Sue. She laughed. "He could be building churches in Africa and you'd find a way to criticize him."

"If he were building churches in Africa, I'd be looking for some kind of flimflam. He'd have some kind of secret connection to the company providing the building materials or something. No, he's just no good and that's all there is. It makes me feel all sick to my stomach to see Evelyn making the same mistake again."

"You should do something about it," said Tudy.

"Rabble-rouser." Ben grinned as he got up and headed back to the kitchen.

"I just like to stir the pot," said Tudy. "It entertains me and my life hasn't been much fun lately."

"I'm going to do it," said Cherry. "I'm going to get some dirt on that Adam and show Evelyn what he's really like. Before it's too late and she marries him a second time. I'm just not going to be able to plaster a happy smile on my face for *that* wedding."

"Uh-oh," said Flo. "Don't look now, but Evelyn is in trouble again with Adam's ex. I guess Evelyn wasn't able to leave the building before Miss Thing came up to talk to her."

Naturally, thought Lulu, all the Graces turned and looked on cue. There was no such thing as "don't look now" for them.

Evelyn was, you could tell, trying to keep her patience. She really did behave like the lady she was, thought Lulu. But she was clearly biting her tongue.

"What's her name again?" asked Lulu. "Seems like every time she comes in here, she's stirring up trouble."

"It's Ginger," said Flo. "She's legally separated from Adam, but they're still married. Once Evelyn came back on the scene, he dropped Ginger like a hot potato. But they were already separated then—so it's not like Evelyn stole him away. Anyway, Evelyn is an ex of Adam's, too."

Ginger, a salt-and-red-haired woman with what must have been a good figure that was now sagging a bit with age, had both hands on her hips and her angry face was too close to Evelyn's.

"Her beef should be with Adam," said Peggy Sue. "He's the one who ditched her, not Evelyn." She absently reached for another bite of her corn muffin.

"This just illustrates the point I was making," said Cherry. "The guy goes through women like yesterday's newspaper." They all watched as Ginger continued giving Evelyn a piece of her mind. Although it seemed to be more of a large chunk of her mind. Apparently, it suddenly occurred to Evelyn that she didn't need to listen to the woman and she finally walked out the door of the restaurant.

Ginger looked frustrated at having her diatribe thwarted. Looking around the restaurant, she spied the table with the Graces. "Shoot! She's coming over here now," said Flo.

"All right, ladies. Let's show her what good manners are all about," said Lulu.

"All we need is a big scene at Aunt Pat's." Cherry glumly rested her helmeted chin on her hands. "The perfect way to end lunch."

It was just another example, though, of why Cherry was glad she wore a helmet. You just never knew when some jealous, vengeful redneck was going to approach you at a barbeque restaurant and give you hell.

"Y'all are friends of Evelyn Wade's?" Ginger demanded, hands on her hips again.

"Yes, we are," said Lulu, shoulders squared. "And I think you know her, too?"

"I do. But our acquaintance is no pleasure. I know Evelyn as a man-hungry home wrecker."

The man-hungry part might be right, thought Lulu. "Evelyn explained to us that y'all were actually already separated when she and Adam started seeing each other. Isn't that the case?"

Ginger's lips poofed into a pout as she considered the validity of this statement. "That part is true," she said grudgingly. "But he and I were working it out. We were trying to get back together and make the marriage work until Evelyn showed up. And I did tell her," said Ginger in a malicious voice, "that it was all about the money.

Adam is always distracted by bright, shiny objects dangling in front of him."

"And you're *upset* that you're not seeing this guy anymore? Seems to me you should be giving Evelyn a medal for getting him out of your hair," said Cherry with a snort.

"That's my own problem and none of your business. I love Adam. We've been together a long time. But I warned Evelyn away and I'll tell you the same. Adam isn't going to do any of you any favors."

"What does that mean? Adam isn't going to do us favors? What are you talking about?" asked Lulu, frowning.

"He's not the kind of person you want to get friendly with," said Ginger.

"Well, I know that," said Cherry in a dry voice. "But I thought that was because he was a slimy freeloader."

"He's more than just a slimy freeloader. He's also a restaurant critic. Have y'all heard of that Eppie Currian?" Ginger grinned unpleasantly. "I can't believe nobody else knew that. And he sure blasted Aunt Pat's this morning," she said with a sly look at Lulu.

Tudy struggled to her feet. "That guy with Evelyn? The pretty boy?"

She got up in Ginger's face. Actually, she towered over Ginger, looking down at her from her nearly six-foot height.

"It wasn't just a review. It was an evisceration. And you *like* him? You think you *love* him? He destroyed my husband's business that he'd been building up his whole life."

Ginger shrugged, but she did step back from the fire-breathing Tudy. "I just wanted to let you know what you were up against, that's all. Maybe you better warn off your friend, like I just warned you. Geez, no good deed goes unpunished," she said, turning as Cherry stood up, too.

Lulu took a deep breath. "I don't want any trouble here at the restaurant. You've warned us off. Now shoo!" Ginger looked at Lulu uncertainly. "Shoo!" repeated Lulu, making the appropriate shooing hand motions to reinforce her words.

Realizing that she was clearly in enemy territory, Ginger made a huffy exit.

Lulu watched her as she left. "Y'all, I just don't have a good feeling about this," she said, shaking her head. "We've got Evelyn's boyfriend/ex-husband/whoever stirring up passions at every turn. And now Ginger clearly blames Evelyn for all her troubles."

Cherry said fiercely, "Don't worry yourself over it, Lulu. We'll figure out a way to get through to Evelyn about the mess she's heading into. Especially since she's completely clueless about how dangerous Adam Cawthorn really is."

Early that evening, Peggy Sue, Cherry, and Lulu rang Evelyn's doorbell. Peggy Sue rested against one of the huge white columns on Evelyn's verandah. "I don't know how I'm going to be able to prop my eyes open all the way through Bunko. I'm completely wiped."

Lulu said, "You do look pretty worn out. What did you do this afternoon after I saw you?"

"Oh, I cooked for the next week and froze it."

"Girl!" Cherry shook her head. "I feel like such a slacker next to you."

Lulu said, "No wonder you're all worn out! What kinds of things did you cook?"

"Well, you know my Grayson loves his Southern cooking. So one of the things I cooked was some bacon meatloaf. Anything with bacon in it is Southern, you know."

"Wouldn't that be hard to reheat later?"

"I make it in muffin tins. That way I can just pull two or three out for each serving. It's much easier that way," said Peggy Sue.

"Pure genius," said Lulu. "I hate cooking for one, but there are some days that I just *have* to have a good meatloaf. I'm going to try your tip tomorrow night."

Evelyn opened the front door. "Come on in, y'all. Sorry it took so much time to get to the door." She was dressed in blue jeans and a tee shirt. Lulu blinked at Evelyn's makeup-free face.

Cherry stared at her. "You sure don't look like somebody about to go out for an exciting night of Bunko. You don't even have your eyelashes on."

"Bertha called me a few minutes ago before I finished getting ready. She said that Charlton had acquired this really revolting stomach flu. I gathered she thought the sound effects wouldn't be conducive to a fun night of Bunko. And nobody else stepped forward to host it. Want to just hang out here, instead? You could just bring in the food from the car. I guess we're going to be eating us some spinach dip and appetizers and gossiping ourselves silly."

"I'll get the Vidalia onion dip out of the car," said Lulu.

Evelyn perked up. "That sweet dip? That I ate the whole bowl of last time? Oh, we're going to have a party, y'all."

Which they did for a little while. But Cherry got into Evelyn's chardonnay a little too much and it emboldened her to say, after a short spell of sober hesitation was overcome, "That awful woman came over to talk to us today after you left Aunt Pat's."

The other ladies froze.

"That Ginger? She spewed her venom your way, too?" Evelyn's face grew splotchy. "It's none of her business anymore. What was she telling y'all? That Adam just wants to date me because of my money?"

"Actually," said Cherry, "she did *mention* that. But then she also told us that Adam was that vicious food critic who's gone around ruining everybody's restaurants. Eppie Currian. I thought Tudy was going to hunt him down and shoot him on the spot. And it was a good thing that Ben was in the kitchen and didn't hear her."

"No, no. She's lying. Adam was a restaurant *owner*

when we were married. He doesn't know how to write a lick."

"Well, he must've figured out how to. Ginger sounded pretty sure about it." Cherry leaned over, picked her helmet off the floor, and put it in her lap as if it might come in handy.

Evelyn stood up, swaying a little. "I need to go freshen up my drink. Anybody need anything?"

"I think I *need* something, but I'm the unlucky driver, so, no," said Peggy Sue with a face.

Cherry jumped a little as her phone started buzzing. She read out the text message there. "Guess what, y'all. I just got a message from Flo. She was out on Beale Street picking up some takeout and she saw Adam there with some other woman! He was smooching on her and everything." She squared her shoulders. "I think we need to get over there. Evelyn's not going to dump this guy until she sees him cheating on her with her very own eyes."

Lulu pursed her lips doubtfully. "I don't know, Cherry. It sounds like a hurtful way of showing her the truth about him. It sounds like she really cares about him."

"Lulu, I promise you it'll be the only way to get rid of him. Otherwise who knows what will happen? You know how she gets these crushes on men. And she doesn't think a thing about getting married. She could end up tying the knot with this guy! On the spur of the moment, on a complete whim, she could hurry him into a divorce and start setting up nuptials for them. No, we've got to nip it in the bud before she gets even more attached."

Evelyn walked back in the room with a full glass of chardonnay and a wary expression.

"Go put on your eyelashes and slap some color on your face, Evelyn! We're going out to paint the town," said Cherry.

Chapter

3

The rain had finally stopped and Beale Street was alive with people. Neon lights illuminated the street below, blues music spilled out the doors of the restaurants, and people jammed Beale, carrying cups of beer in their hands. The restaurant hawkers stood outside the doorways of the restaurants, calling out the specials and the bands playing to passersby.

"I think," said Cherry, "that we should start out at the Alley Cat. Just for something a little different." She fingered her helmet as if trying to decide whether or not she should be wearing it.

Evelyn raised her eyebrows. "That is a little different. Usually we start out at Aunt Pat's."

Lulu jumped in, saying, "We were all at Aunt Pat's earlier, though. Or maybe we can finish up the evening there if we want to."

"Fine with me," said Evelyn, shrugging.

Lulu had an ominous feeling as they walked into the Alley Cat. She was never a fan of confrontation and wasn't totally sold on the idea that this was the best way to convince Evelyn that Adam was no good. After her eyes adjusted to the dark, she saw the place was packed with people. And two of those people were Adam and a bleached blond woman wearing L'Oréal's entire makeup collection on her face at one time.

Evelyn froze in her tracks. Lulu, Cherry, and Peggy Sue didn't say a word as Evelyn processed what she was seeing.

"That's funny. I thought Adam was going to spend tonight at home while I was at Bunko."

Evelyn was still clearly trying not to believe what she was seeing. Then Adam leaned over and kissed the heavily made-up blonde on the neck. Lulu winced. That wasn't something that could easily be explained away.

Evelyn walked with great dignity over to Adam, who, unfortunately for him, didn't see her until she was right in front of him. The other ladies hurried to catch up with her.

"Ginger was right. About *everything*," said Evelyn. "And I was right the first time around—when I divorced you."

Adam shrugged. "If that's what you want to think."

"It's not what I *want* to think. But it's the truth." Now Evelyn was really getting worked up as she saw the food and drinks in front of Adam and his friend. "This is what I gave you money for today? This?"

Her voice had risen as she spoke. Now people around them were getting really quiet and craning their necks to look over at them. Cherry put her helmet on, nervously. Lulu saw someone who looked like a manager watching Evelyn and Adam from behind the bar.

"Don't call me, don't come by, don't talk to me. I never want to see your freeloading self again. I could string you up by your cheating neck."

"Let's just leave, Evelyn," said Lulu, pulling at Evelyn's arm.

The manager came up to them. "How about if y'all talk about this outside," he suggested. "It'd be a more private location to air out any problems you've got." His voice was soft but firm.

"That won't be necessary," said Evelyn huffily. "I don't have anything else to say to this scoundrel."

The silence was heavy in Peggy Sue's car on the way back to Evelyn's house. Cherry looked guilty at having gotten Evelyn so upset (but also pretty satisfied with the result). Peggy Sue was just focused on the road and sitting real close to the steering wheel because, once again, the rain was pouring. Evelyn was so mad she was shaking, and Lulu was trying frantically to come up with something to say. Something that didn't have anything to do with what had just happened at the Alley Cat.

Evelyn finally broke the silence. "Stupid! I just can't believe how *stupid* I was. Everybody kept telling me that Adam was up to no good. I even *divorced* that reprobate once myself. I just couldn't see what was right in front of me—that he was just freeloading."

"What I don't understand," said Lulu slowly, "is why Adam even *needed* the money. If he's that restaurant critic from the paper, then he must be doing really well. *Everybody* in Memphis knows her—I mean him."

Evelyn said, "The reason you don't know why he needed money, Lulu, is because you're always satisfied with what you've got. You're content. But people like Adam are never satisfied; they always want more, no matter how much they have. And the newspaper wouldn't be paying him all that much. All they're doing over there is slashing jobs and cutting costs and trying to keep afloat. Maybe he's famous, in an anonymous way, but he's probably not making a lot of money out of the gig."

"At least," said Cherry, "you can wash your hands of him. And you didn't have to marry him again to find out what a bum he was. Think how expensive that divorce could have ended up being with him as greedy as he is!"

"The only problem?" said Evelyn in a curiously quiet voice. "I want to wring his neck."

"Listen to this, Tudy," said her husband, Oliver, for at least the tenth time that morning. "The number-one reason that the economy faltered during the second quarter of the last . . ."

Tudy gritted her teeth. She'd had thirty years of happy marriage and she'd be damned if it was all going to go up in smoke because of Adam Cawthorn's snarky carping and their restaurant's failure. What Oliver needed was some focus. Like another restaurant job.

She *had* to cut him off. Having the entire edition of today's paper being droned out at you before your second cup of coffee was absolutely unacceptable. Oh, she'd been a good sport about it for the last couple of weeks, but enough was enough.

"Oliver!" she said. He stopped short, mouth still held slackly open and a surprised look in his kind eyes. Now that he was looking at her, she forgot what she was coming up with as a diversion. "Have you . . . Well, have you thought about what I was talking to you about yesterday?"

Oliver looked blankly at her.

"You remember," she said impatiently. "A new restaurant. There's this great location that's opened up right off Beale Street. I think we'd get a lot of foot traffic there. And we could . . ."

He held up a thin hand, stopping her before she could say anything else. "Tudy, it's no good. I *told* you it wasn't any good. That lady just eviscerated me in the paper. The same thing is going to happen again. This time the review will read something like, 'Second Try Falls Short for Oliver Hatley.' It's just not going to stop. It feels *personal*."

Tudy made a face at the word "lady." "Well, one thing I can tell you. It's no lady writing these reviews."

"Right. *Woman*, then. Whatever."

"No, I mean the restaurant critic is a *man*. It's Adam

Cawthorn. I just found out about it yesterday when I was hanging out at Aunt Pat's."

"You *know* him?" Now Oliver's quiet, sensible demeanor had disappeared, replaced by a fury that Tudy had never seen before from her mild-mannered restaurateur.

"Here, honey," she said, handing him the paper. "Can you tell me some more about what happened in the second quarter?" But it was too late. Oliver had already stormed out.

"What is it that you want?" demanded Big Jack. It was better, he decided, to get mad than reveal how baffled and desperate he felt right now.

"I want you to throw the election. Or enjoy knowing that I can throw it just by a few words to the right people. And believe me, I do know who those right people are."

Big Jack swiped at a trickle of sweat that coursed down the side of his beefy face. "So I've been messing around a little bit on my wife. These days, that's not enough to throw a whole election, Adam. I've built myself a platform. I've made the rounds. People in Memphis *know* me."

"How many politicians that you know of have been completely ruined by 'messing around'? More than we can count on two hands. It seems to indicate, to the electorate, a stunning lack of judgment. No, I'd take a bet that your political career, as you know it, would be over. For good."

Big Jack lifted up his palms in supplication. "So what is it you *want*? That's all I'm asking. Are you looking for money?" He knew, deep down, that it was definitely money Adam Cawthorn wanted. And that was worse than political favors. Because money *never* stopped. He'd be paying out for this mistake with that girl for years. And this guy had very expensive tastes—you could tell just by looking at those fancy leather loafers.

Adam gave an unpleasant smile. "I was going to put it a little differently. That I needed you to back me in a business venture that was going to require some regular payments in cash. But, since you like putting things in such a blunt way—yes. Yes, I am looking for money."

Big Jack had never paid anybody to keep quiet about anything. He was a good old boy who played up the fact that he was no slick politician—but a real person with real faults. It was one of those qualities that he thought endeared him to the voters: he was an everyman. He'd agree that cheating didn't really fall in the everyman category—at least not one that most men were going to admit to. He was going to have to figure this out. 'Cause he was damned if he was going to put this pretty boy in loafers for the rest of his political career.

Cherry rang Evelyn's doorbell and waited. A few minutes later she buzzed it again. She'd seen the Navigator *and* the convertible in the driveway and knew darned well that Evelyn was home. And doing her best to avoid her. Cherry had a strong suspicion that Evelyn was working her way through a gallon of chocolate mint ice cream. And she might possibly need rescuing.

Finally the front door opened, revealing Evelyn's housekeeper, Tommie, with a disapproving frown on her face.

"What in the name of goodness are you thinking, Miss Cherry? You think we're deaf or something? Most folks take a hint and leave when nobody answers the doorbell."

Cherry shifted uncomfortably. "I thought maybe the doorbell was broken."

"And why exactly would the dogs have been going berserk, then, every time you pressed that button?" Tommie put her hands on her hips and cocked her head to one side, challengingly.

"Okay! I admit it. I wanted to bug y'all so much that you'd just give up and open the door. Which seems to have worked."

Tommie still looked fierce, so Cherry said in a low voice, "I know how upset Evelyn was last night when we saw Adam at the restaurant. I feel a little responsible because I'm the one who dragged us out there. And I had a feeling we were going to run into him and another woman."

"A feeling, huh?" asked Tommie. She relaxed her stance a little, though. "I never did like that Adam. Not even when Miss Evelyn was married to him. Always sneaking around. Taking things. I'd reach into the silver chest to set a fancy table and half the family silver would be gone. That dog would take a handful of silver off and pawn it. No, I was glad she found out what a devil he is before she ended up married to him again."

Cherry's mouth dropped open. "And you didn't tell her about it?"

"Oh, I told her allll about it, Miss Cherry. But she'd just shrug those shoulders of hers and act like it didn't make a bit of difference to her. 'I never did like that silver pattern, Tommie.' Or else she'd claim that she'd told him it was okay to do it. When she's under that man's evil spell, she's *really* under it."

"Well, I'm glad the spell is broken—for now, at least. I thought I'd drop by and just commiserate with Evelyn for a little while. You know—share some of that ice cream tub she's probably halfway eaten."

Tommie drew herself up to her full height of five feet. "*Ice cream*? You think this is an *ice cream* kind of a problem? No, ma'am. After your heart's been ripped out of your chest and trounced a few times, it's surely not an ice cream matter." She motioned Cherry inside the tremendous atriumlike entranceway and Cherry took in a deep breath.

"Pecan pie," she breathed.

"And not only pecan pie. There's a peach cobbler in the oven, just getting golden right now. And then, if it's necessary, I'm going to pull out the big guns and make a Mississippi mud pie."

Cherry said, "You're a wise woman, Tommie. Emergency measures are definitely in order. I think one of your famous Mississippi mud pies might just fit the bill. And I'm such a loyal and dedicated friend that I'm going to stick around and make sure that every last crumb of that cobbler is eaten, too."

Evelyn was in her bedroom, a huge room with the biggest four-poster bed you've ever seen, a rug you could sink into and disappear for good, and a separate sitting area. Evelyn was reclining on a divan with a blanket over her legs, looking for all the world like that old movie *Camille*. Cherry expected Evelyn to give a weak cough any minute.

But Cherry soon realized that Evelyn wasn't just putting this on. She was mad, madder than Cherry had ever seen her. "I . . . well, I thought I'd help you eat that pie," said Cherry, in a small voice.

They sat quietly, eating, for several minutes. Then Evelyn said, "You know I'm going to get him back for this."

Cherry jumped, thinking at first Evelyn had said she was going to get *her* back. "Oh. You're getting Adam back? Evelyn, this just doesn't sound like you. Usually you can just rise above it—just let the jerk go. Good riddance, right? Next thing you know, you'll have a brand-new relationship with somebody great. Just forget about him." She nervously fingered the chin strap of her helmet. Yes, it was still there for protection if she needed it.

"It's not like the other times when I've parted ways with somebody. This is *personal*. I was falling in *love* with Adam again. And he didn't just cheat on me—Lord knows I've been cheated on before in seven marriages— but he *cheated* me. He took my money and told me he was going to do *one* thing with it and ended up using it to squire sleazy women around town on my dime. No, he's going *down*, Cherry, and I've got a few ideas on how I'm going to do it."

Evelyn gulped down a couple of mouthfuls of peach cobbler, chewing it viciously while Cherry felt that sick feeling in the pit of her stomach grow.

Adam opened the front door of his apartment and tried closing it again. "Oh no," he groaned.

Ginger blithely ignored Adam's unsubtle attempt at escape. "Hey there! I brought you over your favorite supper—shrimp and grits. And it's still warm. I even brought over a couple of plates so you and I could eat together." She gave a hard laugh.

Adam looked coldly at her as she tried to push by him into his apartment. "No, I don't want you coming inside, Ginger."

She chose to ignore this, too. "Okay—so we're dining alfresco? I can deal with a patio meal." She shifted the Pyrex dish, then strode to a small bistro-style table and the two chairs with cracked paint in front of the apartment. "It's a nice enough day." Now her voice was gravelly and impatient again. "Come on over, Adam, and have a seat. I don't have all day and I want to talk to you."

Adam pushed his front door back open and looked longingly inside before closing it again, swearing under his breath, and walking over to the table. He wasn't one to turn down a free meal, and Ginger—for all her shortcomings—really did know how to cook. She placed a large helping of shrimp on his plate. It was still steaming and the creamy texture he preferred. The shrimp were large, tiger shrimp, and the grits had bacon crumbled in. He'd have to remember to tell her the relationship was over *after* he finished eating. He ate a big forkful.

Ginger gave him an appraising look. "I'm here to let you know, Adam, that I forgive you."

He raised a blond eyebrow. "Forgive me for what?"

"Don't be stupid, Adam. I've forgiven you for cheating on me, of course. I know the only reason you went out with Ms. Moneybags is because you wanted money. The woman was a freaking ATM, wasn't she?" Ginger snorted and Adam winced at the sound.

"It was *a* reason. It wasn't the *only* reason."

Adam was getting tired of this conversation. He hadn't realized that Ginger was going to prove this determined and unshakable or he'd never have gotten married to her to begin with. The problem all started when Ginger had pretended to be wealthy to impress him. He believed that she was a frugal heiress, which was why she chose to live in a modest house in a modest Memphis neighborhood. The truth was that she was a complete phony. He'd wanted out as soon as he'd realized her lie.

"Ginger, what you need to get through your head is that we were over even before I started dating Evelyn again. And now it's even *more* over." He took a large bite of the shrimp and grits, spearing a huge prawn and gulping it down before Ginger fired up and something horrible happened to the food.

Seconds later, he stared sadly at the plate of food that Ginger pushed onto the ground as she rose to her feet, face florid. "You're going to be sorry for this, Adam Cawthorn. You'll be sorry you ever heard of me."

But he already was.

Holden Parsons, considering his tremendous love of food, was unfortunately not a very creative cook. In fact, he mused as he heated up a baked potato to heap a can of baked beans on, he was a very pedestrian cook. His happiest days were when he was eating the best food in Memphis on the newspaper's dime. His stomach growled as he remembered all the fine dining he'd done in the past. Ribs at the Rendezvous. Supper at the Peabody. He sighed. When you were out of work, you couldn't keep a caviar budget anymore. Even if he *could* cook, he wasn't going to be able to afford the food he really craved. The newspaper had never paid very well and he hadn't ever been that much into frugality, either. He'd basically ended up with a potatoes and beans budget.

Technically, ten thirty was a little early to be eating lunch. But Holden figured an early lunch was allowed, considering he'd had a meager breakfast at five o'clock A.M. He opened his pantry. Great. No beans left. He could have sworn there was a can hiding in the back there somewhere . . . but no. He looked behind the box of instant grits, the instant mac and cheese, and the Pop

Tarts. No beans. He opened his refrigerator and discovered the dollop of sour cream he'd left had gone even more sour than it was when it had started out. Now there was really no recourse. He was going to have to go to the grocery store. He pulled on a tired-looking bow tie and pulled a comb through his sparse white hair. A plain baked potato was simply not going to cut it. He didn't care *how* little money there was in his bank account.

The first person he saw when he walked into the Kroger was Ben Taylor. He winced. He'd had a hard enough day without running into Ben. He'd become great friends with him during his restaurant critic days and Ben was always good for a free lunch (with a couple of extra cornbread muffins to snack on later). When Holden had found out he'd lost his job at the paper to some anonymous, sniping female critic (who he was sure was both younger and better-looking than he was), his first stop had been Aunt Pat's. He'd been in shock. He'd had that job, had *loved* that job, for the past twenty years. He knew the city of Memphis and its food backward and forward, in and out. When Ben had taken a break from the kitchen and come out and given him a commiserating hug, Holden had—to his complete embarrassment—broken down and cried on Ben's shoulder. He didn't really want to think about that today. Not when he couldn't even successfully cobble together a lunch of baked potato and beans.

He hurried into the canned vegetables aisle, but Ben had already spotted him. And it looked like he had something on his mind. Ben's face was splotched with color and he strode up to Holden, looking extremely agitated. Without sparing any time on pleasantries, he launched right into what was on his mind.

"Holden. You'll never believe what I found out today. You know that harpy restaurant critic? Eppie Currian?"

Well, naturally. Eppie Currian was the whole reason he was foraging for a can of baked beans at the Kroger. He nodded.

"It's not a harpy at all. It's a *man*. And what's more, it's Adam Cawthorn."

Holden frowned, trying to place a face with the name.

"*You* know," said Ben impatiently. "Evelyn's new, old boyfriend. The pretty boy who's always hanging out with her at the restaurant. He used to be her husband, she wisely divorced him ages ago, and now they're dating again."

Holden grew very still. "The blond man?" He'd seen him right on the way to the store. He lived in the same apartment building, and Holden frequently saw him when they were parking their cars.

"That's the very one. I tell you, I could just wring that guy's neck, and I know you could, too. Did you read that review he did on Aunt Pat's? It was like a punch to the gut. And the hack comes to Aunt Pat's every day practically. If he hated the food *so* much, then why keep coming? Naw, I think he just likes making everyone's life miserable. You know, even though Aunt Pat's is in its third generation, the review *still* had an effect on our business?"

Ben was too keyed up to notice how oddly white that Holden had turned. Or the fact that he was working hard

not to throw up. Fury had that odd effect on him. And
vomiting on Ben, after having sobbed on him the last
time, was not what he wanted to do. But he wasn't hearing a word of Ben's tirade now—he was so focused on
trying to keep the sudden, overwhelming hatred under
tight control.

"I know. I shouldn't take it personally, right? I knew
you'd say something reasonable like that, Holden.
You're always such a good guy. But I can't *help* but take
it personally. 'The barbeque's texture is the consistency
of sandpaper. Good thing the tea is good—you're going
to need gallons of it to wash the meat down.' Grr!" Ben
clinched his fists together.

Holden pressed his lips together.

"I knew you'd say that. I knew you'd want me to be
a professional about it. And now that I think about it, I
guess you knew all along who the critic was—you were
just being a pro and keeping quiet about it. That was
real decent of you, considering he booted you right out
of your job.

"Okay." Ben gave a heaving sigh, then thrust out a
beefy hand. "Sorry to vent like this, Holden. You're always a gentleman. Great role model. Thanks. I'll . . .
uh . . . leave you to your shopping." He looked doubtfully
at the baked beans can in Holden's hand. "You know
you're always welcome to red beans and rice at Aunt
Pat's. On the house. Or baked beans—your choice."

As Ben stomped back to his shopping cart with Adam
still on the brain, Holden gripped the can of beans until
his fingers were white.

The lunch crowd was gone, the restaurant tidied up. And it was time, after a couple of hours of holding court in the dining room, for Lulu to put her feet up and relax for a little while. At two thirty every afternoon, Lulu had a standing appointment with the rocking chairs, some iced tea, and the Labradors, B.B. and Elvis, on the restaurant's front porch.

Lulu plopped down in one of the big, wooden chairs. The spacious porch was one of Lulu's favorite parts of Aunt Pat's. It held several picnic tables and three rocking chairs with high backs and checkered cushions. At night in good weather, they'd stack up the tables and chairs and the bands played right there on the porch. The succulent smell of barbeque mixing with the bluesy music pulled people off Beale Street and right into the restaurant.

Right now, though, the porch was nice and quiet. There was a lull on Beale Street, too, as people headed back to their offices or hotel rooms with full stomachs after a big lunch (there wasn't any such thing as a small lunch on Beale). The large ceiling fans rotated lazily. Lulu leaned back in the rocker and nodded off to sleep.

It seemed like just seconds later, but it was more like forty-five minutes, when the screen door's banging slam woke Lulu up with a start. The school bus had dropped off her granddaughters, Ella Beth and Coco, at the end of the street. Every day, Ben and Sarah's girls spent their afternoons at the restaurant—doing homework, replenishing the paper towel rolls on the tables, and generally being good stewards of the Aunt Pat's legacy.

Nine-year-old ponytailed Ella Beth was the perpetrator of the slamming screen door, but it was practically impossible to upset Lulu. Ella Beth threw her arms around Lulu and Lulu gave her a sleepy hug back. "I am *so* glad to be at Aunt Pat's and away from school!"

Lulu pulled back and studied her face. "Did something bad happen at school today?"

Ella Beth's twin, Coco, walked onto the porch more sedately. Coco, whose *real* name was Cordelia, as she liked reminding everyone, was nine going on twenty-one. She leaned over to pat B.B., who gave her a sloppy Labrador kiss that made her squeal. Wiping it off with her sleeve, she said, "Nothing happened at school. Nothing *ever* happens at school. But we had a bunch of pop quizzes today and Ella Beth didn't know her facts about the water cycle. So it wasn't that great of a day for her."

Ella Beth made a face at Coco and said, "Sassy!"

Lulu winked at Ella Beth. "We all have days like that, don't we? Ella Beth, I can go over your notes on the water cycle with you later so you'll ace the next test."

Ella Beth gave her another quick hug. "Sounds good, Granny Lulu. But can I go out and play first? Sitting still all day gave me the fidgets."

"Where are you going—down to the river?" The Mississippi River was just a few blocks away and was Ella Beth's favorite place to go. She'd take a fishing pole some days, some chalk for drawing on others. There were always people to watch, too. Ella Beth loved writing notes in her detective notebook about the people she saw by the river. Lulu figured that Ella Beth was either going to turn into a police officer or a writer.

"No snack?" asked Lulu in mock horror. "I made cheese straws."

Coco gave a delighted gasp. "The spicy ones?"

"The spicy ones. With jalapeno pepper mixed in. Just the way y'all like it."

The routine was a snack on the porch, a talk about their day, and then some homework before it was time for chores around the restaurant.

Ella Beth shook her head, already running outside, screened porch door giving another resounding bang. She turned around on the stairs, "Will you come with me, Granny Lulu? To the river?"

Coco said, "But can I have a snack, Granny Lulu? We had lunch hours and hours ago."

Lulu hesitated. The girls' mom, Sara, who waited tables at Aunt Pat's, had gone back home for a short break before the evening rush. "Sure, sweetie. Let me just fix Coco a little snack first, okay? Then I'll be right over there."

Lulu took the cheese straws out of the tin she'd stored them in. She put a generous amount on a plate, poured a tall glass of milk, and brought them out to the porch for Coco. "How did everything else go at school today, sweetie?" she asked.

Coco shrugged. "It was okay. Just school stuff. John Rotola got in trouble again for not paying attention in class. Pretty normal."

"And the bus ride home was fine?"

"It was okay."

Lulu was beginning to think that everything was

okay with Coco. She was about to walk out the door when Coco actually casually volunteered some information. "I saw Daddy arguing with some man while we were on the bus *going* to school this morning, though."

Lulu stopped and turned half around. "What's that, Coco?"

"Daddy. He was yelling at some man and waving his arms around. It was embarrassing. A kid on the bus was like, 'Isn't that your dad?'"

Coco gave a melodramatic shudder and took another bite of her cheese straws. They were rapidly disappearing along with the creamy milk.

"This man—do you know who he was?"

Coco looked thoughtful. "I don't know his name or anything. He's been in the restaurant before, though. You were talking to him."

Adam? Lulu wondered. And if Ben had been arguing with him, she could just imagine what it was about. She knew that Sara had filled Ben in about Eppie Currian's true identity.

Lulu suddenly felt uneasy for some inexplicable reason. "I'm going to go ahead and catch up with Ella Beth, Coco."

Coco tilted her glass back and finished the last bit of her milk. "I'm all done with my snack, so I'll come, too, Granny Lulu. I want to take my Frisbee with me. Ella Beth and I have gotten really good at throwing it—I wanted to show you."

The two took a left off Beale Street and went down the sidewalk to the Mississippi River. Coco had opened up a little bit more and was now prattling on about her day at school and who she'd sat with at lunch and played with at recess. Lulu tried to focus on Coco, but she kept thinking about Ben. Why didn't he say anything about his argument with Adam when she'd been talking to him in the kitchen? She knew Ben had been furious about the bad review Aunt Pat's had gotten in the newspaper. She guessed that fury all came back to him when he found out the restaurant critic's real identity.

Coco stopped suddenly as they walked and grabbed Lulu's arm. Her face was pale and pinched looking. "Something's wrong with Ella Beth." A frisson of fear went up Lulu's spine at Coco's tone. She'd never discount that twin connection between Ella Beth and her sister. They both ran toward the river.

Chapter 4

The street dead-ended at the water. Ella Beth walked stiffly toward them, face white enough for her freckles to stand out in sharp relief. "Ella Beth! Ella Beth, what's wrong, sweetie?" Lulu pulled Ella Beth into her arms, rubbing her back as if to warm her up. Despite the heat, the little girl was shaking. Lulu looked over Ella Beth's head and froze as she saw Coco had gone down the hill near the river. "Coco!"

Coco spun back around quickly and stumbled back up the hill. "It's *him*," she gasped. "It's *him*, Granny Lulu!"

"Him?"

"The man. The man I saw. The man Daddy was yelling at this morning. He's dead."

Lulu staggered over to a nearby park bench, legs seemingly not eager to respond, still clutching Ella Beth, and now Coco, fiercely. Lulu's mind was whirling and, oddly, the first fully formed thought she had was fury at the damned man for dying somewhere where children could come across his body.

She fumbled in her skirt pocket for her cell phone, fingers jabbing at the buttons. "Ben. Get Stanley to cover for you in the kitchen if you have any orders up and come down to the river. The girls are down here and we've . . . run into a problem. Hurry."

Lulu put down the phone and pulled her grandchildren close to her in a tight hug. "It's okay," she crooned and rocked as she waited for Ben to get there.

She had no faith in her ability to pull both girls back up the hill leading to the restaurant. No matter—Ben was already there. He must have run the whole way down, despite those extra twenty-five pounds he was always talking about shedding.

Ben's shaggy eyebrows were drawn together ferociously. "What the hell is going on?" he panted, drawing up close and looking the girls over quickly. "Are they sick?"

Lulu nodded her head in the direction of the river. "Over there. See for yourself," she said in a murmur.

Ben walked down the small hill, through the trees, to the Mississippi—until he stopped with a jerk and hurried back up the hill, looking grim.

"Come on, girls. I've called Mama and she's on her way back to Aunt Pat's. Y'all got your Frisbees?" He turned to look at Lulu as he walked away. "You've got a phone call to make, too, right?"

Lulu nodded. "I'm going to call Pink Rogers. I've got his number in my cell phone."

"You're not going to just call 911?"

"Pink will take care of it," said Lulu evenly. Pink was a police officer who'd been a regular at the restaurant for the past ten years. He was a fit and trim two hundred and fifty pound, six feet seven inch man—and she would feel a lot better knowing he was there with her. Plus, somebody was probably going to have to ask Ella Beth some questions about finding the body and she wanted Pink to be around.

"Call him now, will you? And come on . . . you need to come up, too. I'm not leaving you down here with—that—by yourself." He didn't voice his thoughts that the murderer could still be lurking nearby, but Lulu was able to pick up the message.

She trailed behind Ben, calling the policeman. "Pink? It's Lulu. I need your help."

In no time, the Memphis police department had cordoned off the area where Ella Beth had discovered Adam's body. There was a forensics team there, walking around in what looked like spacesuits while they gathered bits of evidence.

Sara had stayed at Aunt Pat's with the girls, letting them zone out on television in the restaurant's office. Lulu and Ben stood outside the taped-off crime scene with Pink, who was off duty and able to get right over there. Off duty, Pink wore the pastel button-down shirts he loved and which had given him his nickname.

Pink spoke with some police buddies at the crime scene and then walked back to Lulu and Ben. "It's Adam Cawthorn. Y'all knew him, right?"

Lulu and Ben nodded, keeping silent.

"And Adam didn't just drop dead over there by the river. He was shot."

"I'm thinking," Ben said, "that he hasn't been over there long. That this must have happened pretty recently."

Lulu looked sharply at Ben. He knew Adam hadn't been dead long. Ben had had an argument with him that very morning, when he'd still been very much alive.

Pink said, "It sure looked like a recent crime scene to me. I just hate that little Ella Beth had to come across it. I hope it doesn't scare her off police work for good. I know how much she loves playing detective and I kind of had a hope she might go into the force when she grows up."

They quietly thought about Ella Beth for a minute. "What . . . what was that all over him?" asked Ben.

Pink shook his head. "That was weird, wasn't it? It looked like a bunch of baked beans to me."

Lulu frowned. "Like he'd thrown up his lunch?"

"No. More like he'd spilled beans all over himself or something. Kind of odd for that guy—I never pictured him as the clumsy type. And he didn't seem much like the baked bean–eating type, either, come to think of it."

None of it added up to Lulu, either. Why wasn't Ben

saying anything about having seen Adam that morning?
Why was Adam covered in beans? What in the dickens
was going on?

The Memphis police did an excellent and sensi-
tive job gently questioning Ella Beth. Lulu wasn't surprised, of course, when they discovered that Ella Beth
knew nothing at all that could help them out. She'd been
playing with her chalk, drawing pictures on the pave-
ment where the road ended. Then she'd gone down the
hill to the river to throw some sticks in and see how fast
the current was going. That's when she'd seen Adam.
Lulu felt a pang when Ella Beth sadly said she'd thought
at first it was a grown-up taking a nap—but she'd thought
it was a weird place to sleep. Ella Beth had crept closer
to the body and seen who it was and that he was dead.
She didn't see anyone else around her until Coco and
Granny Lulu had come running up to her.

Ben's wife, Sara, had silently sat, nervously twisting
strands of her strawberry blond hair around a finger and
listening to Ella Beth talking to the police. From time to
time she leaned forward in her chair in the restaurant's
office to listen closer to Ella Beth's small voice. She and
Lulu shared winces a couple of times.

The interview seemed like it was wrapping up. Sara
murmured to Lulu, "I think it's time for me to take the
girls home. Can I give you a call later when it's all settled down a little?"

She stood up, her bigger frame looking solid enough

to handle any trouble that came its way. Sara pulled Ella Beth into a strong embrace. "You ready to go home, pumpkin?"

Ella Beth nodded, rubbing her eyes. The little girl seemed exhausted, although it was only five o'clock. Sara rubbed her on the back. "Wait for me out on the porch with Coco and the Labs, okay?"

"I've called Tina in to work tonight, so don't worry a bit about coming back to wait tables—we've got plenty of help. Tina needed the extra hours anyway. I was going to just let Stanley cook for Ben tonight, but Ben is already in the kitchen cooking away." Lulu lifted a shoulder in a confused shrug.

"I think cooking is therapy for Ben, Lulu. He can put his troubles behind him in that kitchen and forget everything but the food. *Please* don't send him home, okay? He'll drive me crazy there and won't have anything to do but pace around."

"Ben can cook to his heart's content, Sara, until we shut down for the night. Then *he's* probably going to shut down for the night. He's got to be worn slap out. I know I am."

After Sara left with the girls, Lulu walked around the dining room for a while, chatting with customers. But her heart really wasn't in it. When the band set up on the screened porch, she set herself up in a small corner to let the blues music drift over her for a few minutes. The singer's low, crooning voice was a comfort to her. There was nothing like hearing the blues to feel your own cares melt away.

Having friends around you helped, too. As her old friends and regulars, Big Ben, Buddy, and Morty, came through the porch door, she stood up to give them a big hug. "Let's go inside so we can talk," she said, motioning to the dining room. The music, beautiful as it was, was too loud to talk over.

The friends settled into a large corner booth. "I believe I'm going to *have* to order up a beer tonight," said Morty. "It's absolutely necessary after the day I've had."

Buddy gave him a look. "You got nothing to complain about, my friend. We're still alive and kicking, aren't we? At our age, even getting up out of the bed in the morning is a reason for celebration."

The retired blues trio was an excellent example of healthy, active octogenarians. "Y'all are so energetic you wear me out," said Lulu with a tired laugh.

"Now you are a mere child compared to us, Lulu. Twenty years younger than us. I remember being in my sixties and I felt like I could still move me some mountains," said Morty.

"That's true," said Big Ben, nodding sagely.

"And—to correct Buddy—I'm not saying that *in general* I have complaints about my life, y'all. I'm saying that today has been a trial." Morty gave Buddy a cool look.

Lulu hid a smile. She knew the kinds of things that Morty found annoying.

His beer arrived at the table and the men placed their food orders (which the waitress pretended like she didn't already know; the men always ordered the same meals every day). Morty took a sip, paused, and said, "It's that blasted computer."

Now Lulu couldn't hide her smile anymore. Morty dearly loved his computer—until it acted up on him. Then it was the devil's handiwork.

"My grandkids got me on one of those social media sites. You know the kind? Twitbook or something like that?"

Something like that. Lulu nodded.

"They said it was the best way for me to keep up with them. They like to put pictures of their babies up there, stuff like that. So they put my picture up there, showed me how to use it. Then I started getting all these *friends*."

"And this is a *bad* thing?" Buddy made a scornful face. "Having friends?"

"These are not really friends, though, Buddy. These are *Twitbook* friends. So they're people that maybe you couldn't stand when you knew them back in school. Maybe they stole your lunch money or tied your shoelaces to your chair in study hall. But now they've found you, and they've forgotten all about how nasty they were to you back in the day. And then you're stuck! You don't want to be friends with them because there's a part of you that still wants to clean their clock. But there they are, acting like y'all are the best of friends. And now you're finding out what these people had for breakfast this morning or that they're going to get their oil changed or anything like that. When actually, you really don't care if you never hear from them again."

"Do you absolutely have to be their friend?" asked Lulu. "Can't you just ignore the friend request?"

"These people are persistent! Very persistent. They are determined to have a bunch of friends and they'll hound you until you finally give in. And now my news feed is full of who they're becoming friends with and what they're doing. And all I wanted was to see baby pictures!"

Morty took a big, soothing gulp from his beer.

"What's worse? I started e-mailing an old girlfriend of mine: Priscilla. And then I e-mailed something that she must've taken the wrong way—you know how it's hard to tell people's intentions from what they write? So now she's all huffy and upset with me and I haven't even done anything! It's just that dern computer."

A dreamy look came over Morty's face. Big Ben, Buddy, and Lulu winked at each other. They knew that look well. With Morty, it meant he was about to spin a heckuva tall tale.

"I remember back when we were touring on the blues circuit," he said in a soft voice that deaf Big Ben had to lean forward to hear.

"Blues circuit," said Buddy with a derisive snort. "Like it was something really big."

"Friends really were friends back then. And there wasn't any e-mailing back and forth nonsense or sharing what you ate for breakfast that morning. I had this lady friend, Rachelle." His eyes had a faraway look. "And she was gorgeous. She and I were a great couple and she *always* knew exactly what I was thinking. We were simpatico!"

"Funny how I don't remember Rachelle," said Buddy musingly. "Considering we spent all those years on that blues circuit, you know."

"That's probably because you were tipsy half the time, man."

Big Ben gave a big guffaw before he changed the subject. He'd been around those two long enough to know when they were getting too scrappy with each other. "Lulu, why don't you tell us about *your* day. You were looking pretty weary when we first got here."

Lulu rubbed her eyes. "You just won't believe it when I tell you."

"Does it beat Morty's bad-day story?" Buddy's eyes cut over at Morty.

"Let me tell you and you decide."

So Lulu quietly filled them in on what had happened that afternoon. Her monologue was punctuated by "isn't that a *shame*s" and "good Lord a-mercies." When she finished up, they sat there for a second, munching on their barbeque ribs and thinking.

Morty said, "How about if I order *you* up a beer, Lulu? That's the most horrible story I've heard in a long time. The poor babies, having to discover that no-good scallywag like that. He couldn't even die with any sense of decency. I never did like Evelyn's friend. He was surely someone who needed killing."

"I don't feel bad for him at all," said Buddy. "I think

he got what he had coming to him. But I feel awful for Ella Beth and Coco, having to find him."

"Case closed!" said Big Ben in his booming voice. "I know who did it. I know exactly who killed Evelyn's buddy. I just haveta turn him in."

Chapter 5

Lulu knit her brows. "Who?"

"That fella whose restaurant went under. You know, the one who had the restaurant all those years until he got that nasty review. He was so mad about losing his restaurant that he was practically spitting nails. His wife is in here all the time."

"Tudy's husband? Oliver?"

"That's him!"

Lulu took a thoughtful sip of her iced tea. "I just don't know, Big Ben. I have a hard time picturing him as a killer. He's such a quiet guy."

"Don't you know it's always the quiet ones you've gotta watch out for? All those folks who say, 'I lived next door to Jack Spratt for thirty years and I had absolutely *no* idea he had five people buried smack dab in the middle of his backyard.'"

"Maybe." Lulu squinted doubtfully at him.

"Or it could be Tudy what killed him," said Morty. He thoughtfully chewed a big spoonful of his red beans and rice. "She was awful upset yesterday. Remember? Cherry was telling me that she was fussing to y'all because he was driving her crazy. She wasn't ready for her husband to be home all day long, no sirree. Messing with her daily routine. Compromising her afternoon nap. He was making her life *complicated* and it was all that Adam Cawthorn's fault."

"So Tudy killed Adam because she was furious that Oliver was reading the entire A section of the newspaper aloud to her? I'm not so sure about that as a good motive," said Buddy.

"But having her naps compromised sure sounds like a motive to me!" said Lulu with a laugh. "Y'all should know about that. You get set in your bachelor ways and then suddenly someone's there changing your day around. Wouldn't it drive you crazy? You know about that, don't you, Buddy?"

"Well, that is true. I dearly love Leticia, but when we started dating, she suddenly wanted to change the kind of clothes I was wearing." Buddy looked down at his plaid, button-down shirt.

"You sure look good to me," said Morty, leaning back and scrutinizing Buddy's attire. "Looks clean. No buttons missing. What did she think was wrong with it?"

"She said they looked like an old man's clothes," said Buddy glumly.

"And aren't you an old man?" barked Big Ben.

"Haven't discovered the fountain of youth, have you? Nor Leticia, either."

"That's for sure. But she took me shopping anyway. Now I've got all these polo shirt things. And golf shirts. And then some blazers for getting dressed up." Buddy sounded glum. "But I only pull them out of the closet when I know I'm going to be hanging out with her."

"That right there is exactly the reason I'm not crying into my beer that Pricilla is upset with me. 'Cause she could've gotten all messed up in my business. One second you're having a nice little dinner for two at a bistro. The next second you're in line at the Steinmart with a whole new wardrobe of plaid golf shirts and tight jeans."

"Getting back to what Lulu was saying, though," boomed Big Ben. "Let's ruminate on this for a minute. I really do think that Oliver killed that critic. And I'll tell you why." He leaned across the table and tapped a long, arthritic finger on the red checkered tablecloth. "I saw him. I saw him talking to Evelyn's guy at lunchtime. And wasn't he furious?"

"Where was this?"

"Well, today is the day that I meet with my bridge friends. We'd played bridge this morning, then went out to lunch together. We were over at that new place—the New Blues Café. And then we saw Adam come in. And right on his tail was Oliver. And he was a righteous mess, let me tell you. His shirt tail was half tucked in, his face was all red and splotchy. And it looked like he was *crying*."

The other guys murmured over this. Crying was not

something that this generation of males did very much
of.

Big Ben continued, "And so Adam laughed right in
his face and gave him a shove right out the door of the
restaurant. And I guess Oliver was so humiliated that he
did leave. But he was just *about* as mad as anything. I
think the tears were tears of anger." He ruminated for a
minute. "But it was just about the most exciting thing our
bridge club had ever seen. Even more exciting than when
Rupert McDonnell stepped on Ida Harvey's cat and the
creature leaped at him, scaled his head, and skidded off.
Tore that toupee right off his bald head."

"I bet he looks better with that wig off," said Buddy
thoughtfully.

Lulu didn't spend long talking after that. The
blues band had done an excellent job of pulling customers off Beale Street and soon the staff was all jumping
to keep up with the orders of barbeque sandwiches and
ribs. Lulu's mind was still caught up thinking about
Adam Cawthorn. She'd really like to believe that Ben
had nothing to do with his death. *Surely* he didn't. Did
he?

After the crowd had finally all pulled out, the tablecloths had been taken off, and the tables scrubbed down,
Lulu sat down on the front porch for a few minutes with
a tall glass of sweet tea, then Cherry opened the door.
But if she hadn't had her Elvis helmet and wildly bright
and mismatched clothes on, Lulu never would have

guessed it was Cherry. The usual bounce in her step was missing and she seemed oddly subdued.

"Hi, Lulu," said Cherry, looking around her surreptitiously. "You out here on the porch all by your lonesome?" Cherry turned slowly in a 360, looking all around the screen porch before finally ducking down to the floor and looking down under the table.

"Mercy, Cherry! There's nobody else out here, not even any little people. It's past closing time. Who did you think might be lurking around under the porch tables?"

Cherry's face turned about as red as her shirt. "Well, now, don't take this the wrong way, Lulu, but occasionally Ella Beth likes to do a little detective work. I just love that little girl to *death* . . . but I wanted to talk with you a few minutes in private."

Lulu wrinkled up her forehead. "I really would be worried if Ella Beth were out here at midnight. Of course, honey! Tell me what's on your mind."

"All right." Cherry sat down in a rocking chair, took the cap off a bottle of water, and took a couple of sips. "Sara called me a while ago and told me all about y'alls' rough day. And I was at home thinking about it." She took a deep breath. "Evelyn killed Adam Cawthorn."

"*What?*"

Cherry nodded and absently took off her Elvis helmet, cradling it protectively in her lap. "That's right. She shot him dead. I know it. And now I don't for the life of me know what I'm going to do about it."

"Cherry are you *sure*? How do you know?"

Again with a deep breath. "I know because I felt so

terrible about how I'd practically dragged her out to Beale to see Adam cheating on her. I went over and visited with her this morning to help cheer her up and to tell her that Adam was just a scummy slug and not to spend a moment worrying over him. She was eating herself into a coma with the most *delicious* food that I think Tommie has ever cooked. But then she told me that he was 'going down' and she had some ideas on how to do it!" Cherry finished her summary with relief and looked anxiously at Lulu.

Lulu rocked for a minute quietly with her eyes closed. "Cherry, I think you're misinterpreting what she told you. You know how Evelyn is—she probably had some mischief in mind to play on Adam. Maybe she was going to post an embarrassing picture of him on the Internet, or go tell Ginger that she'd caught him cheating on *her*, too . . . something like that. I just don't see Evelyn Wade taking a gun to somebody. I don't care how mad he made her."

Cherry whispered, "But what should I *do*? Should I ask her about it?"

"Why don't we give her a little time to process all this before we start asking her questions. I'd hate for her to get her feelings hurt thinking that we don't trust her."

Cherry shifted uncomfortably in her rocker. "Okay, Lulu. I'll go along with that plan for a little while. But if she doesn't say something about where she was or what she was doing when Adam Cawthorn was killed . . . I just don't know how I'll be able to look Pink in the eye the next time he's in Aunt Pat's."

Cherry seemed to have calmed down. What Lulu

thought actually happened, though, was that Cherry had just transferred all her stress to Lulu. When Cherry finally left to get back home, Lulu decided she might as well end her night with a heart-to-heart with her son. Although Lulu's neck and shoulders were bunched with tense muscles, she felt herself relax a little as she walked through the door of the kitchen.

The Aunt Pat's kitchen was her favorite place on earth. She'd grown up there with her maiden aunt showing Lulu how to cook as she perched up on a high stool, and her aunt even let her help make the corn muffins for their guests while they worked. A bunch of shiny copper pots hung from the ceiling and there was also a pegboard with pots—installed as soon as Aunt Pat saw that her beloved Julia Child had set up a pegboard system to organize her cookware.

Ben was still cleaning up the kitchen, perspiration forming beads on his forehead as he worked. The kitchen was still toasty from all the cooking. He looked up briefly as his mother walked in and sat at a wooden stool at the long counter. Finally he stopped his scrubbing and looked at her. He pulled up another stool and plopped down on it with a gusty sigh. Now that he'd sat down, he actually seemed to realize how tired he was. He rubbed his eyes with a beefy hand.

"Long day, wasn't it, Mother? I guess I should be heading back home to make sure the girls are okay."

Lulu said, "I'm sure Sara would have called you if there'd been any problems. It was an awful shock for them, but children are so amazingly resilient."

Ben nodded and took a big swallow of some sweet tea he'd had beside him as he cooked.

"But I did want to ask you about something." Lulu sat up straight on her stool and leveled Ben with a look that made him squirm a bit. "Coco told me this afternoon that she'd seen you having a big argument with Adam Cawthorn when she was riding the school bus this morning. That's why she recognized the man after Ella Beth discovered his body. Now"—she raised a hand up as Ben opened his mouth—"I'm aware you knew he was the critic who wrote that ugly review on Aunt Pat's. I'm sure Sara told you all about it. And I know that's what you must have been arguing about with him. Maybe it wasn't even an *argument*, maybe you were just telling him off. But I need to know, honey, if things went any further than that."

Ben looked even more exhausted than he did before Lulu started talking to him. "That snarky review of his just killed me, Mother. It was like he was sticking sharpened steak knives right into me. And knowing that he was happily eating at Aunt Pat's practically every day, gobbling down the very food he'd bashed, practically licking his plate clean? After saying all that stuff about my cooking? It made me see red. I couldn't stand not letting *him* know that *I* knew who he was. That he was no Eppie Currian. And that I never wanted to see him in Aunt Pat's again."

Lulu straightened out a wrinkle on her floral dress, then looked Ben right in the eye again. "And that's all there was to it?"

"That was *it*." But Ben didn't quite meet his mother's eyes. She could swear that there was something he wasn't telling her.

"And you don't know who *did* do it? Because he seems to be a really unpopular man."

Ben gave his head a quick shake. "No clue who murdered Adam Cawthorn, Mother. But I'd like to give him a medal."

Chapter

6

Lulu and Flo rapped on Evelyn's massive, double front doors. They had a big takeout box from Aunt Pat's filled to bursting with cornbread muffins, ribs, and baked beans. Tommie came to the door after a minute. "Ooh, well looka here! Y'all brought me some food."

Lulu hugged her with a free arm. "We brought enough for two, Tommie! You make sure you get yourself a heaping plate of it. I know how much you love the ribs at Aunt Pat's, so I put a bunch extra in there." Lulu looked around Tommie to the cavernous foyer. "Isn't Evelyn around today? We thought she might be feeling poorly after what happened to Adam."

Tommie clearly knew all about it. She nodded her graying head. "That scamp! Yes, Miss Evelyn told me all about it. But she's not nearly in the shape she was in when Cherry was here before. No, she seemed almost chipper about it all. Although she did want to go out and get herself a little bit of stress relief. You know how sometimes you just got to get out of the house?"

Flo said, "Good for Evelyn! What's she doing? Taking a walk? Or did she go to that yoga class she was trying to drag me to." Flo turned to Lulu and said, "Yoga! Can you imagine it? If my body was meant to bend like that, God would have made me a pretzel."

Tommie gave a belly laugh. "No, y'all, she didn't do anything all that healthy. Although she does get on her kicks where she don't eat nothing but seaweed-looking stuff and exercises with a trainer. I do hate it when she gets on those health kicks of hers and I don't get to cook all my favorite foods for her. She's taken off for the spa today. Wanted to do something nice for herself, you know. She's over at the Chic Clique Spa."

"Even better!" said Flo. "I didn't much feel like catching up with her while she exercises, but telling her how sorry I am while I get my nails done sounds like a great plan."

Lulu said sadly, "I don't think you need any beautification effort. You look perfectly put together to me." Lulu looked at Flo's carefully styled bouffant, unchipped nails, and cute outfit.

"Honey, there's *always* more work that can be done!" said Flo.

Lulu looked a little doubtful. "Well, I did want to talk to her and see how she's getting on. I don't know about a spa, though. That's not something I've ever done."

Flo's mouth dropped. "You haven't gone to a spa?!"

"No. I mean . . . I've gotten my nails done at NailPro, but that's just for special occasions. Not an everyday thing."

Tommie hooted. "I have a feeling you're about to get indoctrinated into the finer things in life, Miss Lulu."

"I just didn't know I knew *anybody* who hasn't gone through the primping process, Lulu. I can't spend as much time or money over there as I'd like to, but I'm all about getting a nice facial, or getting a pedicure or manicure. And *some*times, when I'm really stressed out from the wedding planning? I even go get myself a massage. Not the long ones because they're too expensive, but the fifteen minute ones still do a ton of good when your neck is all twisted up in knots," said Flo.

"I bet those weddings *do* get stressful," said Tommie with a whistle. "Sometimes someone will call me up to do some baking for one. I'll do some cakes or some tea sandwiches or something like that. But dealing with those brides is some kind of stress. They're little ego monsters, they are."

"See, you shouldn't have told me you do weddings, Tommie!" Flo gave a wide grin. "Now that your secret is out, I might get in a pinch and have to give you a call. And things do get pinched sometimes, believe me. You wouldn't believe the caterers who just don't show up for a reception. No call, no nothing! Just didn't feel like crawling out of the bed that morning, I guess."

Lulu could tell Flo was starting to get worked up again. "Come on, Flo. Let's check out the Chic Clique.

Sounds like you have some stress that needs to be worked out, too."

Lulu had, at first, felt just a little bit uncomfortable going into the spa. She'd originally thought she was just going over to Evelyn's to share some ribs with her friends. She smoothed her bright floral dress self-consciously. With her carelessly twisted-up hair bun, hit-and-miss approach to makeup application, and fondness for happy-looking print dresses, she felt just a little bit shabby when the glamorous young women at the reception desk greeted them.

But Lulu had to hand it to the staff at the Chic Clique Spa. They knew how to make you feel like a queen. The heavily made-up receptionist beamed at Lulu and Flo. "How are you ladies today? Having a special day out?"

Flo sashayed up like she went to Chic Clique every day of her life. And Lulu was starting to think that maybe she did. Come to think of it, Flo always did look just perfectly turned out. Lulu thought she just spent a lot of time on her appearance in the morning, but maybe she came to places like these every once in a while.

"We *are* having a special day, actually," she said with a quick smile for the receptionist, whose gilded nametag said "Brittany." "We're here meeting a friend of ours, too. Evelyn Wade."

"Oh! Mrs. Wade. Yes, she's one of our favorite guests. She's just finishing up a treatment, I think. I'll check and see where she is now. And ladies, we *are* running a special for our guests today on salt glows. I know that's what Mrs. Wade started out with today." Brittany noticed Lulu's confused frown. "It's *wonderful*. You'd just love it. It's a sea salt rub. It exfoliates you and just takes all those tired cells off. It's *heaven*."

Lulu thought it sounded just a little uncomfortable for her. She was about to pooh-pooh the whole thing when Flo stepped in. "I think, since we've joined our friend so *late* today, you know, that we'll just stick to the basics. Is Evelyn going to end up with a manicure and pedicure?"

It just so happened, Brittany assured her, that she *was* going to. Right after her massage therapy. Flo lifted up her hand like she was in a classroom. "Me! Right here. You can sign me up right now."

And so it happened that Lulu reluctantly found herself being led up a curving staircase to a luxurious changing room, where she put on the thickest white robe she'd ever seen in her life. She felt like she'd followed Alice through the looking glass. "Herbal tea?" asked an attendant, when Lulu stepped out into the hall. Lulu shook her head and smiled.

Flo was already robed and waiting for Lulu on a bench outside one of the treatment rooms. "You are just going to *love* this, Lulu! You'll be a spa addict now—you mark my words!"

The treatment room had a waterfall at one end and was designed as a group room. Evelyn was already under a crisp white sheet, getting a massage. "Hey, girls," she said in a sleepy voice. "What a nice surprise! A spa day with my friends. It's perfect."

Lulu said, "Well, we went by your house to check on you and bring in some ribs from Aunt Pat's and Tommie said you were over here. So we thought we'd catch up with you here."

The massage was unlike anything Lulu had ever experienced. The female masseuse was getting out all those knots and kinks from Lulu's shoulders from years of restaurant life. This *could* end up becoming a habit.

Flo said in a muffled voice, "This is just exactly what I needed, y'all. Between my batty brides and my cat . . ." Her voice trailed off like she didn't even want to think about it.

"What's going on with your cat now?" asked Evelyn. "I told you that was one crazy critter. Don't you know somebody who lives out on a farm or something? That animal would be loving life if he could hunt rodents on a farm all day."

Lulu smiled to herself. The cat's name was Dammit— for a good reason.

"Well, I don't know, Evelyn. I love Dammit. He's a good cat—he just does crazy things sometimes. Like yesterday—he jumped out at me from a doorway when I was walking down the hall."

"I think that's kind of cute, Flo," said Lulu.

"Oh, it was cute except it scared the fool out of me. And I just happened to be carrying a cup of coffee in my hand. And wearing a really nice dress because I was getting ready to have a meeting with one of my brides." Flo sighed. "Maybe some of the stain will dry clean out."

For a few minutes the ladies enjoyed their massage, until Flo said, "Lulu and I—well, and all the Graces— were just wondering how you were handling Adam's death. And to tell you we were sorry about it."

Evelyn made a muffled sound of outrage. "Please! Not while we're paying to be relaxed. We're working out our tension and toxins! Later."

After the massage, the ladies padded over to the nail room for manicures and pedicures.

It was there, after they'd picked out their nail color and were soaking their feet, that Evelyn said casually, "I trashed Adam's condo yesterday morning."

"What?" All the women in the nail parlor leaned forward.

"I did. And it felt great. The jerk. And I wasn't sorry at all to find out that someone shot him, although y'all were real sweet to come over and comfort me and bring ribs and all."

Lulu looked apprehensively at the manicurists. Evelyn waved her hand. "Don't worry about these ladies. They know *all* my secrets, don't y'all?" The well-groomed ladies laughed and nodded.

An elegant brunette said, "We wouldn't be working here long if we spilled all the secrets we heard every day."

"And we hear some doozies," said a blond girl as she applied lotion to Lulu's hands and forearms.

"They know I wouldn't hurt a fly," said Evelyn. "Of

course, Adam was worse than a fly. He *needed* to be stomped. But I didn't do it."

The Greek chorus of manicurists echoed Evelyn's opinion of Adam.

"So you went over to his house and just started wrecking it?" asked Lulu.

Flo said in a voice of hushed admiration, "Boy, oh boy!"

"I surely did. Well, I started out really normal, right? I knocked on his door, rang his doorbell. I was just as polite as you can imagine. I have my *manners* and *breeding* you know. But then he didn't answer. No breaking in was necessary because I had my key still. So I just let myself in," said Evelyn.

"One of the things that just bugged me to pieces about Adam was his obsession with neatness. Now, I'm *neat*, but I don't have to have my pantry stacked up just so and my rugs lined up just right. I don't need everything in my refrigerator to be lined up with the labels facing the front. Just open the door and shove it in, is what I say." Evelyn frowned in impatience at even the memory.

"Amen!" said one of the Greek chorus girls.

"When we were married, he used to fuss at Tommie for not nesting the pots and pans just so in the cabinet."

"The gall!" said Lulu, thinking protectively of her own kitchen. "The kitchen should be set up the way the *cook* wants it."

"Exactly! So Tommie set him straight on that one. There was no way she was going to have some man coming in and messing with her kitchen. Anyway, so I was remembering the way he was and looking at all his obsessive-compulsive neatness. All the perfection. All the alphabetizing of the spice cabinet. And suddenly, the devil got into me. I yanked at his desk drawers, threw papers out, willy-nilly. I took his throw rugs and crumpled them up—I knew *that* would drive him up the wall."

Lulu beamed her admiration at Evelyn. "Good for you! I'm glad you didn't let him get you down." She was hoping this tale was going to end with Evelyn's little fit of vandalism and not end up taking a detour down the winding trail of murder.

"My favorite part? Since he's such a foodie, I figured I'd ruin whatever he had in that fridge of his. So I pulled out his soy sauce bottle and shook it over everything in his fridge! His mayo, salads, mustards, even in his milk and cheeses. It was *so* funny."

Flo said, "What made you finally put on the brakes? I'd think that once you got started vandalizing somebody's house that it would be hard to stop."

Evelyn got this misty look on her face. "Girls, it was actually my experience with Alpha Delta Pi that stopped me. They had all this leadership training at the University of Alabama. And I thought about that." She choked up for a second and put a hand to her throat. "They always said to be strong. They wanted us to be strong women *always* and to never lower ourselves to be common. I thought I was borderline on 'common,' so I stopped sloshing the food around. I'd *made* my point.

"But I did have one other thing to do. I decided to

change his answering machine message and make it just as snarky as all his restaurant reviews. So I got on there and said, "Adam can't come to the phone right now. He's busy writing nasty reviews for the paper under his Eppie Currian pen name. Got a restaurant? Want to send some hate mail? Here's Adam's address. . . ." Evelyn still looked pleased with herself.

Lulu said, "Well, honey, that was right ingenious of you. But did you have to get your revenge on the very day the man was murdered?"

"I don't know anything about that. Well, I did know he was murdered, because after I left his condo I went down to the river for a few minutes to catch my breath. You wouldn't believe how much energy goes into trashing someone's property. A *lot*. So I went down to the river and sat on the bench down there. Until something red caught my eye. And you can imagine what *that* was." Evelyn fidgeted for a minute. "Damn, I want a cigarette. Gave those things up years ago, but I still crave them like crazy."

"The only thing I feel bad about is your girls finding that body, Lulu. I should have just called the cops right then. Only thing is that I'm going to be suspect number one. I was clearly upset with him. I left evidence of my visit all over the place—answering machine included. I didn't want to be at the scene of the crime, too, you know? I just had no idea those little girls would find his body."

Evelyn leaned back in the chair and rested her head

on the headrest. "Nancy, do you think you could pull out that chardonnay I know you have in the lounge fridge? I think we need just a splash of it . . . don't we, ladies?"

Lulu craned her head to look for a clock.

"Now, now, Lulu! Just go with the flow. It's five o'clock somewhere," said Evelyn.

The chardonnay was very cold, just the way Lulu liked it. This had been some kind of day. She'd had no clue when she'd woken up that morning that she'd end up sitting in a luxurious chaise getting a pedicure and sipping chardonnay in the middle of the day. It was a very decadent feeling. And she was surprised to find she liked it.

"The thing is"—Lulu still felt a little self-conscious discussing the murder in front of the manicurists, although they did seem very nice—"is that I was hoping to get some clues as to who might have done this. Here I am, once again, really close to a murder investigation. *I* just want to make sure Ben has nothing to do with this."

"Ben!" Flo gave a gravelly laugh. "What on earth would Ben have to do with this murder, Lulu?"

"Nothing, I hope. But Coco saw him arguing with Adam yesterday morning while she was on her way to school. So there's that. And he sure was steamed about that ugly review Adam gave him. He's been stewing over that since he found out."

Evelyn nodded, thoughtfully. "For a man like Ben, though, cooking is really an art form. He's devoted his life basically to become an expert at cooking barbeque and all the fixings. He's just not going to take kindly to somebody slamming his abilities in a public forum like a newspaper."

Lulu sighed. "That's what worries me. He *was* that upset. He just seemed to take it really personally."

"Well, I can relieve your mind right there, Lulu. You just stop your worrying. Because I know who killed Adam Cawthorn and it sure wasn't Ben."

"Who was it?" Lulu gripped the armrests and pushed herself up so she could see Evelyn better.

"It was Big Jack Bratcher. No, don't look at me like that, Flo! I can promise you that it was. Because when I was in there messing with Adam's answering machine, I heard an old message in his voice mail. It was Big Jack pleading with Adam to meet him somewhere so he could talk to him about the money."

"The money?" said Flo. "What money? What's Big Jack been doing?"

"See," said Evelyn, "this is where I'm wondering if Adam wasn't being a little shady. I mean, we already know he was greedy and that he was a liar and a cheat. It's not too far down that road to becoming either a con man or a blackmailer."

"You're thinking," said Lulu, "that Adam was maybe blackmailing Big Jack over something. Something bad that he knew about him? Considering that Big Jack has invested a ton of money and time into his campaign, I'm pretty sure he'd pay about anything to keep from losing the election."

"That's right. We already know that Adam wasn't ex-actly squeaky-clean. He was basically robbing me of my money while cheating on me with girls. He was greedy and not really scrupulous about where the money came from. Sounds like he'd make a great blackmailer to me."

The door to the nail salon suddenly flew open and Peggy Sue was there, a little out of breath with a rosy glow on her plump cheeks. "Tommie said y'all were over here. Why didn't you call me up! You know Chic Clique is my favorite place in this world, besides the Krispy Kreme doughnut shop. I was worried I wasn't going to be able to catch up with you before you left." She turned to one of the manicurists. "Hi, Helen! Can you paint me with my usual Ruby Slipper nail color? Makes me feel like Dorothy!" She plopped down in one of the vacant chaises and an attendant quickly turned on the jets on the foot bath.

While Peggy Sue was still giving some last-minute directions to Helen about her manicure and pedicure, Evelyn looked meaningfully at Lulu and Flo and made a hushing motion. No surprises there, thought Lulu wryly. Peggy Sue was the biggest blabber this side of the Mississippi. There was a good reason why Evelyn would trust the staff at Chic Clique before Peggy Sue.

"Now, girls, this is living! Well, it is as soon as I get a dab of that wine. Helen, can I have a little? Yum!" Peggy Sue sighed contentedly, leaning back in her chair and holding her wineglass aloft. "To us! And to Evelyn for having the good sense to break up with a murderer."

"No, no, Peggy Sue," said Flo with a little irritation. "*Adam* wasn't a murderer. He was *murdered*."

"Whatever," said Peggy Sue in a bored voice. "Lulu!"

Lulu jumped a little.

"I wanted to let you know that I'm going to set Derrick up. I've got the perfect girl for him to go out with. *Perfect*. It's my granddaughter."

Derrick was Sara's seventeen-year-old nephew. Sara's sister and Derrick's dad had split up, then her sister had up and taken off with another man. She'd asked Sara to take Derrick for her, which Sara had done, for the boy's sake—but then later because he'd become a real member of the family.

Lulu wasn't sure about Derrick dating one of Peggy Sue's granddaughters. He was so *quiet* and serious. He just didn't seem like a good fit for anybody that might be closely related to Peggy Sue. "Well . . ."

"Now, don't be that way! Why . . . do you think she's too young for him? Remember, these are my *step*-granddaughters. And Peaches is almost eighteen."

Flo leaned forward in her seat. "Peaches?"

"That's what we call her. But it's not her Christian name. That'd just be silly. Can you imagine being in God's holy sanctuary with the minister in his robes and the baby all dolled up in an heirloom gown and having the minister baptize you as Peaches? No, her Christian name is . . . well, I'll be hornswoggled. I can't remember it!"

Lulu said slowly, "I'll be sure to mention it to Derrick, Peggy Sue. But you know, he's just so darned *shy*. . . ." And Lulu wasn't sure what he'd think about going out with a girl named Peaches. In Chicago, he was probably used to girls named Crystal and Rhianna.

"And that's the beauty of it! Peaches doesn't have a drop of shyness in her entire body. And since she's new to town and doesn't know many people, she's dying to go out and have some fun. So she's already planning to call him up and issue a special invitation to see that new romantic comedy and have a coffee afterward. It's perfect!"

Poor Derrick, thought Lulu. She could only imagine breaking the news to him. He hadn't dated anyone since he'd gotten to Memphis, but Lulu had a feeling that he was probably the kind of guy who liked to find and ask out his own dates.

Peggy Sue was still getting beautified when the rest of the ladies were done. "At least we got to say hi," said Lulu to Peggy Sue as they walked out.

"Sorry, but I've got to get out of here and enjoy some of those ribs that Flo and Lulu brought to my house. Tommie might eat them all if I don't."

"Party poopers," sang out Peggy Sue. "Don't forget to tell Derrick what I said, Lulu. Let him know that Peaches will be giving him a call sometime this week!"

Lulu winced but smiled.

Chapter

7

As they left, Evelyn said, "Let's go beard the lion in his den. I bet I know just where Big Jack is right now. We can pop right over to the country club and get a Coca-Cola and see him. That's his big hangout, you know. He loves to cut up with all the good old boys at the club. Besides, I want to get the story straight. You and I know that the police are going to end up at my house soon. And I'm not sure I can get the same amount of pampering in the Memphis jail as I just got at the Chic Clique Spa."

Lulu followed Evelyn's Cadillac over to the club. On the way over, they dropped Flo back off by her house. She had to plan a wedding that night and didn't have any time to go running after Big Jack Bratcher.

The country club, thought Lulu, belonged on a *Gone with the Wind* set. It was white and sprawling, with a manicured lawn; a verandah with huge columns; and an immaculate, expansive golf course spotted with retired executives wearing poorly matched outfits.

As Lulu recalled, Evelyn spent a lot of time at the club herself. She'd told Lulu that she spent much of the summer there sunning by the pool, playing tennis with rotating partners on Thursdays, and happily ordering froufrou cocktails there on Friday evenings. Must be nice, Lulu thought a little wistfully as she followed Evelyn in the big, wooden doors.

"Big Jack will be running his mouth in the lounge. I see him there *all* the time," said Evelyn confidently. Sure enough, as soon as they got to the lounge, Lulu could make out Big Jack through the dim lighting, laughing loudly at another man's joke and slapping him on the back. When he saw Evelyn, he left the bar and walked right over. "Why, Evelyn Wade! What a pleasant surprise to see you here today."

His lips twisted with humor and Evelyn said, "Oh, cut it out, Big Jack. You know good and well that I'm over here almost every day. Are you busy shooting the bull? I was wondering if you could spare a few minutes to talk to Lulu and me."

Big Jack was named as much for his presence as his size. He was definitely a big man, but his aura was even bigger. He couldn't hush his booming, rafter-shaking voice if you told him to.

"Well, now, that sounds pretty serious! But seeing how the request is coming from one of my top campaign donors, I just don't see how I can possibly refuse," said Big Jack.

"Let me get you ladies a drink. We just can't face a serious conversation without a little liquid encouragement."

Lulu said to Evelyn, "This is a whole different world for me. Spa treatments in the morning and wine and mixed drinks before it's even one o'clock in the afternoon!"

"Oh, honey, this is nothing. This is just some casual imbibing with friends. You should see Big Jack and me when we really get going. We have such a good time, Lulu. Of course, I do think he's a ruthless killer, but that kind of goes with the political territory."

"Are we going to be able to talk to him privately, Evelyn? Somehow the country club just doesn't seem like the ideal location for a heart-to-heart talk."

"Are you kidding? This place has a million nooks and crannies. Beaucoup conversation areas with leather chairs, Oriental rugs, fireplaces with big oak mantels, and heavy drapes. The staff are like ghosts and they scatter if they ever see someone having a heart-to-heart discussion. No, this is the perfect place to be. If we talked to Big Jack at home, then we'd have to deal with his wife, Lisa."

Big Jack came back with their drinks and motioned them down a long hallway covered with thick carpeting that had a fleur-de-lis pattern. The halls were lined with large portraits of past club presidents—they all looked to Lulu like serious, paunchy, bald men in suits. "Let's go to the solarium," he said. "There won't be a soul in there today. Plus, those birds put up such a racket that nobody can hear a word over them anyway."

The solarium's floors were old brick with cushy Oriental rugs scattered around. The comfortable armchairs' upholstery was covered in warm shades of reds and oranges or floral prints; the walls were floor-to-ceiling arched windows, with potted palm trees between the arches. The ceiling was glass paned, too, with a big chandelier hanging from the center. There was a stone fountain at one end and two large bird cages with some striking tropical birds gazing out. They did chirp and talk from time to time, which is probably why Big Jack thought it would be a good place to have their conversation drowned out. Lulu thought that the water from the fountain provided even more white noise than the birds did.

They took a seat and both Big Jack and Evelyn sipped their cocktails. "Now that we've gotten all civilized," said Big Jack, "why don't you tell me what's on your mind? Is there anything that I can help y'all out with?"

"That's just what I figured you'd say, Big Jack," said Lulu. "Every time I see you at Aunt Pat's, it seems like you're giving somebody a hand with something. But, no, we don't need any help from you today—we had more of a question for you."

He raised his heavy eyebrows questioningly.

"The thing is, Big Jack," said Evelyn. "I was in Adam Cawthorn's condo yesterday—trashing it, actually. And I got on his answering machine to screw up his announcement and I heard your message on there. It sounded like Adam had you over some kind of barrel.

Believe me, I know how he was. I figure the police are going to question you and me and I just wanted to talk with you before they did."

Big Jack frowned. "Forgive me for asking, Evelyn, but what in the hell are you talking about?"

Lulu stared. "Didn't you hear, Big Jack? Adam Cawthorn was murdered yesterday. Shot in broad daylight out by the river."

Big Jack's tanned face turned a little paler. "No, I'm afraid I hadn't heard that." He took a bigger sip from his drink and Evelyn did the same.

"Well, that does make life complicated," he said with a sigh. "Being all wound up in a murder investigation isn't really ideal during a political campaign. But there's just no way out of it. I'll call Pink up and give him my statement and avoid having the Memphis police come to my door. Maybe I can just go over to the station or something."

Seeing that Big Jack was starting to get into PR-recovery mode, Lulu said, "What happened with Adam? Was he trying to blackmail you?"

"Oh, yes, ma'am, you could say that. He had me right over a barrel, just like you said. He was always going out on the town with different ladies. . . . Sorry, Evelyn." Evelyn just pressed her lips together and gave a jerking nod of acknowledgment. "Anyway, on one of his evening expeditions, he happened to see me out there. And I wasn't with Lisa, as you can imagine. I wasn't in a club or anything stupid like that, but I was in a car with a lady and I guess he could tell I wasn't talking politics. He's been trying to squeeze money out of me ever since."

He rubbed his eyes with a big hand. "I don't mind telling y'all about this, because I know it's not going to go any farther than the doors of this solarium. But having *him* know about it—having Cawthorn act all oily, like he and I were sharing a secret—it drove me nuts. But—I didn't kill him. Just like you didn't kill him, Evelyn."

There was a slight questioning rise to the end of Big Jack's sentence. "No, I surely didn't," she answered coolly.

"I know one thing I'm going to have to tell the police. I have a good idea who might have done it. Actually, who *tried* to do it. But I just can't imagine that he actually was successful. Let me explain what I mean."

Big Jack cleared his throat and said, "You know Oliver, my cousin?" Big Jack had at least fifty to seventy-five cousins. Some were closer than others. It was one of the things Lulu thought made him a successful local politician. Half the town voted for him because he was family. And Lulu had heard from some of them who were her restaurant regulars that he did his best to help them out in return, even if it meant giving them a few dollars to tide them over from time to time. She'd always thought he had a heart as big as the rest of him.

"Well, now, he came up to my door this morning,

and it must have been two A.M. Lisa was hanging back, peeking behind me, sure there was some kind of marauder out there or else that we were getting some bad news. But there was Cousin Oliver. Y'all know how he's usually a tidy, straitlaced dresser, right? Lotsa buttondowns and loafers. But he looked like something the cat coughed up, he looked so bad.

"Lisa was half asleep, but she went into the kitchen and brewed up some strong coffee—that Columbian stuff we keep in the pantry. And she made some cheesy drop biscuits that took her just a few minutes, but they were *good*. And Lisa even cut up some fruit to go along with them. I felt like I was having breakfast." Big Jack was fond of his food and was digressing a little from the key points of his story. Since he was talking to two foodies, though, they were willing to cut him some slack. In fact, Lulu made a mental note to ask Lisa about her cheesy drop biscuit recipe.

"Then Lisa goes up to turn back in. She's almost cross-eyed she's so sleepy. But Oliver was still a jittery mess. After a little bit of talking, though, he started to settle down some."

Big Jack paused and took another healthy, restorative gulp of his brandy.

"All the time, I'm really just wondering what Cousin Oliver is doing in my kitchen in the middle of the night. I was sorry about his restaurant closing, and I'd already done what I could to get him a spot at another restaurant—which he took. But then he'd quit it because he just couldn't stand working for someone else instead of having his own place. Which I can kind of understand.

"Finally he told me, 'I killed him.' And he was really broken up . . . shaking and crying and everything else. So I ditched the milk and poured us a strong one instead and brought in a whole box of Kleenex. I thought I might have to start crying, too, if he'd just gotten me involved in this mess even worse than I was in already. And I remembered that damned answering-machine message!"

"So you *did* know Adam was dead, then," said Lulu.

"No—not really. I finally got Oliver to stop with the crying and he just hiccupped every now and then, which was a big improvement. He told me that his wife, Tudy, had let it slip that Adam was the infamous Eppie Currian from the paper. He'd seen red, he said. The anonymous reviewer wasn't even a woman. And the guy had come into his restaurant plenty of times—he was practically a regular. He'd never had a single complaint about the food—except maybe that he wished the portion sizes were bigger because he wanted more. And all the time, he'd been the one who wrote the review that shut them down.

"So he'd looked up Adam's address online and decided to shadow him in his car and I guess have some kind of showdown with him. And, typical Adam, he heads over to Beale Street to grab something to eat. The guy loves his food, you know. So he parks in a parking deck nearby and Cousin Oliver goes right in the deck behind him."

Lulu leaned forward.

"Oliver tails him into a restaurant and confronts him. He told me that he'd really gotten wound up and pretty emotional, so he's half yelling, half crying and letting Adam have it in the restaurant lobby. But Adam just laughed at him and pushed him right out the door and went ahead with his lunch. Oliver paced around Beale Street for a while, deciding what to do. He's in a state. He decides to wait for Adam to come out so he can confront him again. When Adam finally does finish his lunch and leave, Oliver follows him to the parking deck and up the stairs. Oliver yells at him again and Adam just is sick of it by now, I guess. Oliver catches up with him on the stairs while Adam is just verbally telling him what a loser he was and what a loser his restaurant was. He's waving his arms around and steps off balance for a minute. While he's wobbling, Oliver pushes him down the stairs."

Lulu winced. "Those concrete parking deck stairs."

Big Jack nodded. "That's right. So Oliver takes off in a panic and spends the rest of the day hiding out. Makes some kind of excuse to Tudy so she doesn't think he's missing. Then he comes by my place."

Big Jack stopped for a moment and took a sip of his drink. He seemed to be relaxing with the sound of the fountain behind them.

"But he wasn't dead," said Lulu. "He wasn't found there in that parking garage."

"That's right," said Big Jack, pointing a thick finger at Lulu. "In fact, I saw Adam later yesterday afternoon while we were both stopped at a stoplight near Beale. I just looked at the person in the car next to me and, sure enough, it was him. And he looked like he'd been in a fight—he had a bloody nose, and what looked like scratches and lumps coming up on him. Of course, you can also get those injuries falling down a concrete staircase."

Evelyn sat back on the floral sofa. "Well, shoot. I never thought meek and mild Oliver Hatley would have it in him to push somebody down a staircase."

"He must have been so relieved," said Lulu. "I mean, when you told him that you'd seen Adam in the car and he was only banged up and not dead. He must have thought he'd killed him."

Big Jack nodded. "He did think he'd murdered him. And relieved is right . . . he started crying again. Which I sure didn't need. All I wanted was to go back to bed and finally get some shut-eye. This is the first I've heard that Adam is dead. That's bad news for Oliver and me both."

"Mercy!" said Lulu. She mulled it all over for a moment. "On Beale Street at lunchtime there must have been a dozen witnesses to that argument."

"Oh, easy," said Big Jack with a nod of his head.

"And that answering machine message means that they'll want to talk to you, too."

"I'm sure it'll be a nice little chat," said Big Jack, trying to look unconcerned. But he looked glum when he noticed his glass was empty. "Oh, and Oliver was babbling about a blog, too. I guess he must have said something about Adam online. Anyway, the cops will likely make a beeline for the both of us." He lifted his head and looked at Evelyn. "And you, too, I guess. If you've been in his condo and messing around with his answering machine."

Evelyn looked at him coolly. "I'm surprised they haven't come by to see me already."

Chapter

8

Back at Aunt Pat's, Lulu felt like she'd landed back on earth from a foreign planet. Just seeing the cheery red and white checkered tablecloths and the paper towel rolls on the tables was a relief after all the expensive linens at the country club. Between a spa day and drinks at the country club, it had been a most overstimulating day.

Sara took a break from waiting tables and joined Lulu out on the porch. "Lulu, Derrick should be back from school any minute now. I was wondering—do you think something's been bugging him lately?"

Lulu said, "Honey, I've been thinking the same thing. In fact, it's funny you mentioned it to me today because I've planned on talking with him this afternoon. He does ordinarily have a pretty serious look on his face, but I believe his expression has hopped over to the grim side lately. Do you think he's having problems at school?"

Sara's brows drew together in an anxious frown. "I have the hardest time telling! I guess I just don't have good teenage-emotion radar yet, since the girls are just nine. And then I've been so busy between the restaurant and the twins and my art that I haven't really spent enough alone time with him to even ask him about it."

Lulu said, "My problem has been that the boy is wired up. Every single time I want to have a conversation with him, he's got those earbuds plugging his ears up and he's texting something on his phone. And I just know he's blasting rock music so loud that he'd never be able to hear me. But this time I have a plan, Sara. I've reached back in my memory to the days when I had a teenage son myself. I remembered what made me the Great Communicator."

Sara said, "Fill me in on your secret, Lulu! I'm feeling desperate."

"Food," said Lulu with self-satisfaction. "That's the way to get through to a teenage boy. You have the fried stuff—the fried green tomatoes, the shoestring French fries, and the fried okra. Then you have the sweet stuff—the peach cobbler topped with ice cream, the chocolate floats, and the cookies. By this time, they're just spilling all their secrets, they're so desperate to make sure the food supply doesn't get cut off."

"Brilliant!" said Sara. "That's the best plan ever. Because, boy, that child can put away some food."

"And the second part of my plan is to pull those wires out of his ears. There's no way he can listen to my pearls of wisdom if he's got rock music cranked up to full blast.

I'm calling this the Super Grandma approach. Or maybe Rambo Grandma."

"What's on Rambo Grandma's menu today?"

"I started baking over an hour ago and I have some hot gingersnaps, peanut butter cookies, and a sweet and salty trail mix. I'm thinking I'm going to get somewhere with that. And you know that Peggy Sue is setting her granddaughter up with Derrick for a date."

Sara rolled her green eyes. "Lulu, I just don't know if Derrick is date-ready. He's been so withdrawn lately. What kind of a date would he be?"

"He'll be a *great* date. We—well, we just have to work on him a little bit. Get him to smile a little more. Or smile at *all*."

Lulu sat on the Aunt Pat's porch, rocking with great determination in her rocking chair until the wooden floorboards creaked underneath her.

Sure enough, Derrick slouched through the door right after school let out. He was wired up with his iPod and gave her a nod and wave of the hand as he headed back to the office to do his computer work for the restaurant. Then he stopped, drew in a deep breath, and unplugged from his music. He grinned at Lulu. "How'd you know I needed some cookies, today, Granny Lulu?" Lulu smiled at the glimpse of the old Derrick. She'd take any bit of the non-sullen version that he sent her way.

"Oh, we grandmas just know these things, Derrick,"

she said, now rocking gently in the chair and giving him a sweet smile. The last thing she wanted to do was to scare the boy off.

He plopped down next to her and happily took a handful of cookies, plunking them down on a small plate. He took a big bite of his first cookie and his eyes rolled back a little. "Umm!"

Lulu took a deep breath and decided to plunge right in. She knew Derrick was only going to stay put for a few minutes anyway. "Honey, how are things going at school for you lately? You've seemed pretty withdrawn—I was just a little worried about you. You know how we grandmas can be," she said with a laugh.

Derrick's dark eyes looked warily at her over his milk glass. "What do you mean? Like I've been quiet?"

"Don't you think you've been quiet?"

He shrugged and shifted as if he were going to stand up and retreat with his cookies, but then he hesitated. "I dunno. I guess so. It's just that after I got rid of my old friends, it's been hard on me. I don't have anybody to hang with at school. So I'm quiet there and I guess it lasts over to the rest of my day, too."

Derrick's old friends had been the first crowd of kids he hung out with when he moved to Memphis. They were a big reason behind the fact that he'd been in and out of trouble with the law for misdemeanors before cleaning his act up a few months ago. And one of Lulu's happiest moments was when he'd taken to calling her "Granny Lulu" instead of "Lulu."

Lulu nodded. "I know that's tough, Derrick. But you know you've done the right thing—those guys weren't good enough to be your friends. You've got so much more promise than they do."

Derrick snorted, but his face brightened with the praise.

Lulu took a deep breath and seized the moment. "By the way, honey? I don't know if you're dating anybody right now or not"—Derrick's face went from partly sunny to instantly cloudy again—"but you know my friend Peggy Sue? She's got a granddaughter. . . . Well, I guess technically it's her step-granddaughter. But anyway, she was just dying to have you and this step-granddaughter of hers go out on a date."

Derrick opened his mouth up really quickly and Lulu reached across and handed him another cookie to sustain him through the conversation. "Here, honey. Now, I know this is incredibly inconvenient, and I'm so sorry about that. But this little girl apparently just moved to Memphis and Peggy Sue is trying to introduce her around. She doesn't seem to go to your high school."

"Granny Lulu, I just—" He stopped. "I just don't want to ask anybody out right now." He leaned forward and spoke in a low voice. "The whole thing with school, not having any friends? It's—rotten. I couldn't call somebody I don't even know up right now and ask her out."

Lulu could tell that the words were hard for him to say. But this was a boy whose mother had chosen to leave him for some man she was having a fling with. Was it any wonder he was having insecurity issues?

"Well—guess what?" Lulu said in a falsely peppy voice. "Peggy Sue's got it all set up. Yes, she's really quite the organizer. Her granddaughter, Peaches, is going to call you soon and set up dinner and a movie. I think she's one of those really modern girls. She might not even let you pay!" Lulu gave a forced laugh and Derrick groaned.

"I'm so sorry about this, sweetie. Tell you what—I'll find a way to make it up to you, I promise. But if you could go out with her just this one time, it would mean such a lot to me. Peggy Sue is a dear old friend of mine. And maybe? Well, maybe this Peaches is cute. After all, Peggy Sue is cute! Or she *was*, back in the day."

"But you said that Peaches was her *step*-granddaughter."

"So I did," said Lulu slowly. "Well, hon, maybe we can just hope for the best."

Derrick shrugged a thin shoulder, although Lulu could tell he wasn't as unconcerned as he looked. "It's just one date, right? If it doesn't work out, then that'll be it." Derrick took a few big gulps of his drink, then hesitated. "There was one other thing I did want to mention to you, Granny Lulu. While we're having this talk."

"What's that?"

"It's probably nothing. But after what happened with Ella Beth, I thought I'd better bring it up. That guy who was murdered? I was working on the Aunt Pat's blog and Aunt Sara and I figured it would be good for me to see other local restaurant blogs and find out what kinds of things they were doing. And I came across that guy Oliver. You know—the one who had that restaurant that closed down? I know he comes in here a lot, and his wife does. He said all kinds of things on his blog and Twitter page about the dead guy . . . Adam. He acted like he was really steamed. I thought you might want to know."

Another Oliver story, thought Lulu. She was going to have to check out what was going on. "There wasn't anything really crazy on there, was there? Like him admitting he'd murdered Adam or anything?"

"No, there wasn't anything like that in there. But it was like he wanted to ruin Adam's job, you know? Because if all the restaurants knew who he was, it would make it harder for him to review them. Who knows if the paper would even want him? And Oliver had Adam's picture on there and everything. He was really slamming him like he wanted to make it hurt."

Lulu sighed. "I sure appreciate your letting me know, Derrick. I guess the police will end up finding out soon enough and go to talk to him. I guess we have to presume he's innocent, right? But still watch ourselves. There's definitely someone dangerous out there. I just hope it's not Oliver."

Derrick headed back to the office to start on the computer work again, leaving Lulu looking blankly out at Beale as she tried collecting her thoughts. Sara, taking a break from cleaning up the dining room, joined her. "How did it go?"

"It went all right. He caught sight of the food and he sat right down. I think he's doing okay," said Lulu slowly, pursing her lips. "But he's still fighting with that insecurity of his. Who knows—maybe this date will be a good thing for him. But he was worried about that, and worried about Oliver Hatley. When he was looking at other Memphis-area websites to help design ours, he came across all this angry talk from Oliver about Adam Cawthorn and how he'd ruined his life. Derrick was just letting me know."

Sara rolled her green eyes. "Of course Oliver was furious with Adam/Eppie/whoever. We were furious with him for the bad review and he didn't even shut Aunt Pat's down. But I don't see Oliver as the murderer."

Lulu raised her eyebrows. "Who do you think did it?"

"Ginger Cawthorn, of course. And I bet the cops do, too. The spouse is *always* the top suspect in all those police shows."

"But Ginger and Adam weren't married anymore."

Sara shook her head until red spirals of hair tumbled around her face. "They *were* still married, remember? But they'd been separated for a while when Evelyn started seeing Adam again."

"And she sure was mad about Adam dating Evelyn," said Lulu, nodding. "But wasn't she more mad at *Evelyn* than Adam? It seems more likely that she'd shoot a big hole in Evelyn than Adam."

Sara said stoutly, "If we don't buy into that scenario, though, then we've got to explore the idea that some of our friends might be murderers. And I really don't want to go there."

Lulu rubbed at her temples. "It's all making my head spin. Let's talk about something else. Like—the girls. How are the twins doing now?"

Sara smiled proudly and said, "They're doing so much better than I thought they would, Lulu. Kids are so incredibly resilient. I'm not going to say they didn't have nightmares last night—because they did. But I was amazed how well they're handling this."

"What did the counselor say to them this morning?" asked Lulu. "I was busy with customers when y'all came in a little while ago." Sara had taken the morning off and gone to talk to a pediatric counselor with the twins.

"Oh, she was wonderful. Asked them what happened, let them talk it all out of their systems. And then she said all the right things to help them process it and make a little sense out of what happened. I think it helped a lot."

"Do you think I should even mention anything about the murder to them?" asked Lulu.

"They'll probably start talking to you about it, actually. That seems to be where they are in the process right now."

"How're my babies doing?" asked Lulu, giving Ella Beth and Coco big hugs as they came out on the porch. She wasn't really sure exactly how to handle such a traumatic experience, so she was relieved when Coco piped up.

"Pretty good. We had a whole day off from school so we could talk to some lady who was a counselor."

"And the teachers didn't even give us any make-up work!" said Ella Beth. "But I've had some bad dreams, so I guess it's not really been too great."

Lulu nodded. "Well, I wish there was something I could do to make the bad dreams go right away. But I think that as time goes by, they won't be quite so awful." She squeezed both girls' hands. "I do have something to put a smile on your face in the short term. I made y'all some apple pie and some home-churned ice cream to go on top." The twins cheered and seemed to put the murder out of their minds as Lulu brought out two plates heaped with generous portions of hot apple pie and homemade vanilla ice cream.

But after Coco, happy with her full tummy, left the porch to do homework, Ella Beth lingered. "Something on your mind, sweetie?" asked Lulu.

Ella Beth nodded, her thin face serious. "I was watching this movie that was on in the office. And it had this guy who was just a regular guy but his friend got killed."

Lulu made a mental note to monitor what was on the television in the office more often.

"And so he went on a hunt for the guy who killed his friend. He became a totally different person. Because he was '*emotionally invested*,' he said."

"But, sweetie, you didn't even know this man who died. He was a grown-up and honestly, he wasn't even a very *nice* grown-up. So there is really no reason to feel close to him at all."

Ella Beth shook her head. "But the point is, Granny Lulu, that I'm *emotionally invested*. I'm the one who found him. I want to help find out who did him in."

"You didn't mention your idea to your counselor, did you, sweetie? I don't think she'd think this was a great way to handle your shock."

"Actually," said Ella Beth, raising her pointed chin, "the counselor said we were supposed to work out our feelings in a healthy way. This sounds pretty healthy to me."

"Oh, honey. I think she probably meant that you should go to your mama's workshop and throw some paint on a canvas. Or go outside and run around for a while—something like that."

"Finding the man's killer means that everything is all tied up, though. Very neatly."

Lulu was about to quickly squash this idea, but then she looked closely into Ella Beth's pinched face. The little girl had really been affected by finding the murdered man. Maybe, in some ways, just letting her think she was helping put the murderer away would help focus her energy in a positive direction. She obviously wasn't just going to forget the murder and put it behind her. It *wasn't* tidy.

"Tell you what," said Lulu. "Why don't you plan on doing a little investigating. *Just* around Aunt Pat's, Ella Beth. And you make sure you tell me everything you find out, okay? And—you're not going to want to let people know that you're nosing around in this—just to be on the safe side, sweetie. There's obviously a really disturbed person out there."

Ella Beth drew back, offended. "Granny Lulu, I'm not *dumb*. Detectives are supposed to work undercover. And then I'll report everything I find to you. Just like I did the last time when that food-television reporter was murdered."

Lulu had to admit that Ella Beth, despite being nine years old, had definitely helped her out with the last case she'd found herself involved in. Murder. Circling around Aunt Pat's! What had the world come to?

Chapter

9

The next day the lunch rush was bigger than it had been the rest of the week. "I think folks have pushed that review out of their heads," Lulu said to Ben as he grated huge blocks of extra-sharp cheese in the Aunt Pat's kitchen.

"I sure hope so. It's just wrong that one person's opinion could mess up our business for as long as it did. And it wasn't even true! Adam was pigging out on red beans and rice at Aunt Pat's every chance he got." Ben looked steamed just thinking about it as he grated vigorously.

"Well, there's no need to get all fired up about it now, Ben. Adam's not too likely to be writing any more stories in his current condition."

"Yeah. And I just can't seem to summon up an ounce of sympathy for the guy, somehow." Ben saw his mother's worried face and said, "But I didn't murder him,

Mother. You know that's not the way I'd go solving a problem or settling a score. I was set to *expose* him, though. I figured if I let everybody know who he was, then he couldn't go around bashing people's restaurants and putting them out of business—because they'd be on the lookout for him. He'd have no secrets."

"I think Oliver Hatley was beating you to it, sweetie. Derrick was saying that he had blog posts up with Adam's picture and a big story about Eppie Currian's real identity. He was even spreading the news on Twitter."

Ben hesitated. "I was doing more of a word-of-mouth campaign. There's only one thing that worries me. And I don't know if I'm overreacting or what. I mean, it probably doesn't mean anything." He started cracking a couple dozen eggs into a large bowl for the spicy corn muffins.

Lulu put her hands on her hips and cocked her head to one side. "I *knew* you weren't telling me everything. When are you going to learn that it's never good to try to hide things from your mama?"

Ben gave a small smile. "I guess you're right. Anyway, I saw Holden Parsons at the grocery store late in the morning that day Adam was killed. I felt this real evangelical need to tell him Eppie Currian's true identity. I figured Holden had just as much of a beef with Adam as I did. Hell, he probably had *more* of a beef with him—it was Adam's fault that Holden lost his job as the paper's restaurant critic."

Lulu nodded. "Right. I knew Holden was really torn up about that."

"And when I was thinking about it later, Holden

didn't look so hot while I was talking to him. He turned red, green, white—just about every color you can think of. But I was just so focused on *telling* him that I didn't really even notice until later that he was looking sort of sick."

"Well, sure he looked sick, Ben. Holden had no idea you were going to throw that information at him. And it probably brought up a lot of unwelcome feelings."

Ben beat the eggs into some shortening. "True. Yes, that's true, Mother. But then I noticed what he was holding in his hand—a can of baked beans."

Lulu remembered that Holden's body was inexplicably covered in baked beans. "Oh."

"The only reason I remember that is because I said something about it. 'You should just head over to Aunt Pat's for your baked beans fix' or something like that." He sighed. "And there Adam was—murdered and covered with a bunch of baked beans."

"So what are you going to do? Have you talked to Sara about this?"

"I sure did. And she wants nothing more to do with this murder. Bad enough having our little girls discover the body. And the cops will probably end up talking to me about the whole thing anyway—I wasn't exactly spreading a sunshine message about the guy. When they come to talk to me, I haven't decided if I'm going to say anything to them about Holden. I mean, don't you think they'll probably find out on their own?"

"Maybe. Although it's not like those beans are all that distinctive. But they'll probably be talking to Holden anyway, since he lost his job because of Adam. I guess they're more likely to find out about him that way." But Lulu sounded doubtful. "I usually think that honesty is the best policy."

"Me, too. But I think I'm going to hold off on being honest for a little while. I'm not *lying*. I'm just not offering up everything that I know."

The dining room was already full of customers for the lunch rush and the talking and laughing made the volume really loud in the room. But Lulu could still hear Ben's wife, Sara, laughing up a storm as she cut up with some of the Graces, Big Ben, Morty, and Buddy. When Sara saw Lulu, she started getting up, "Guess I better help get some orders to the tables," she said, smoothing down her apron. "We've got a real crowd today, thank God."

"Sweetie, I don't think we need to do a thing but enjoy ourselves. I had two of the girls call and ask me if they could work today—that they needed more hours this week and wanted to make some extra money. I told them that was just fine . . . which ended up being a good thing since we're packed. So let's just have some fun and visit with our friends."

Sara's large frame seemed to relax in her chair a little. "That sounds like a good plan, Lulu. It's been a rough week. Some downtime would be great."

"Where are Flo and Evelyn?" asked Lulu. "They have docent duty at Graceland today?"

Cherry shook her head and made a face. "No. Well,

Flo's meeting with one of her brides for work. But Evelyn? You'll never guess where she is.

Big Ben, Buddy, and Morty seemed to view Cherry's statement as a personal challenge.

"She's buying a third house?" offered Big Ben.

"She's buying a fourth car?" guessed Buddy.

"I got it!" said Morty, managing to snap his arthritic fingers. "She's buying another pair of those fancy shoes that cost more than my car payments?"

"Wrong, wrong, wrong!" sang out Peggy Sue. "She's out with *Ginger*! You remember Ginger? The wronged woman from hell?"

"I can't hardly believe it!" said Lulu. "Why on God's green earth would Evelyn deliberately want to spend time with that woman? The last time they were together, Ginger insulted Evelyn by telling her that Adam was only going out with her because of her money."

Flo nodded her carefully teased head. "Which ended up being absolutely true. So Evelyn felt like Ginger was trying to give her a friendly warning—one that she should have been heeding."

"But she *wasn't*," said Cherry crossly. "She was giving Evelyn a piece of her mind because she'd just been ditched." She stabbed some baked beans with her fork.

Buddy said in a thoughtful voice, "And I keep thinking that Ginger might have killed Adam. Think about it—usually it's the wife or the ex-wife, right? She probably just got fed up with trying to reconcile with somebody who was out partying with other girls. And so she shot him cold."

Big Ben shook his head. "Maybe. But I got my own theory on the murderer." He raised his eyebrows at Lulu and nodded. Obviously, thought Lulu, his money was still on Oliver. That scene at the restaurant had stuck in his mind.

"Maybe," said Cherry, taking a sip of sweet tea. But Cherry gave Lulu a look that meant she was still worried about Evelyn's possible role in the murder.

"Hush! Here she comes," said Lulu, her head swimming with all the suspicions from her group of friends.

Sure enough, in came Ginger and Evelyn, arm in arm as if they'd always been the best of friends. "Hi, girls!" said Evelyn breezily. "Y'all remember Ginger, don't you?"

"And how," mumbled Cherry. Flo kicked her under the table and Cherry grunted.

"Ginger and I have had a wonderful talk and really put all our petty little differences aside. And we found out that we have so much in *common*!"

Lulu raised her eyebrows. "Isn't that nice? What did you find that you had in common?"

"Besides Adam?" said the sullen Cherry. She got another kick under the table from Flo.

"Would you believe we're *both* originally from Tupelo? And we both lost our moms in our twenties? And we both love to eat barbeque best of all!" said Evelyn, beaming.

"That's really wonderful," said Lulu a little flatly. It was hard to garner any enthusiasm for someone who had been yelling at your friend the last time you'd seen her. And who could be a cold-blooded killer.

"You're practically twins," said Cherry. She turned to Lulu and rolled her eyes.

Ginger acted like they were all meeting each other for the first time. "You know I love the food here," she said to Lulu. "This is one of my most favorite places to eat. It's another great thing about hanging out with Evelyn—I have a chance to eat more Aunt Pat's barbeque." She gave a simpering smile and pulled up a chair to join the group.

"The police finished their autopsies and everything," said Ginger abruptly. "Adam's funeral is going to be in a couple of days."

Everyone tried to look appropriately mournful. Big Ben muttered something about being sorry in his gruff voice.

"Evelyn, would you come to the funeral with me? It would really mean a lot to me if you would."

Evelyn looked cross. "Ginger, you're forgetting everything we talked about! The whole point was how scummy Adam was—how he did us both wrong! How we're even *glad* that he's gone . . . and coming to terms with the guilt from that realization!"

Ginger pouted. "I don't care what he was. I loved him! I'm going to love him until the day I die, and no one can stop me. In fact, I'm going to get to the bottom of this murder. I'm going to find out who did him in, believe me. Because he was *going* to get back together with me. Besides, I already have some ideas that I'm going to share with the police soon."

"But we were going to *heal* together, Ginger. Don't you remember? It was going to be therapeutic for both of us."

Ginger shook her head emphatically, reddish gray curls bouncing. "No. I wanted to hang out with you because we could both *reminisce* about Adam. Share our memories and stuff like that. It'll be almost as good as having him around."

Or *better* than having him around, thought Lulu. He really was a stinker.

Evelyn got very quiet. "If that's the way you feel, Ginger, I'd rather not discuss Adam around you. Because I'm not in that stage. You're in some sort of denial phase . . . denial that he treated you like dirt. And I'm in the stage where I'm just trying to deal with the fact that I'm guilty of being happy he's dead. I need to *heal*. But I'll go to the funeral with you. I promise I'll do that."

To Lulu's relief, Ginger didn't want to stay for lunch—she was going to get her hair done so she'd look nice for Adam's visitation at the funeral home. The way Ginger was determined to keep Adam's memory alive, Lulu wondered if she somehow thought she was getting dressed up to look nice for him. Lulu shivered.

As Ginger walked out the door of Aunt Pat's, Sara said, "Evelyn, honey, that woman is creeping me out.

What are you doing hanging out with her when you could be hanging out with us instead? We're a whole lot more fun."

Peggy Sue said, "And she thinks you want to be her little mourning buddy or something. It's just weird."

Evelyn said, "I know y'all think I'm nuts, but it's part of my healing process. This has been a really traumatic time for me—going from feeling like I was the Queen of the Universe when I was with Adam, to getting cheated on and scammed out of money, to having Adam be murdered, and then to having the police peg me for a suspect. Hanging out with Ginger makes me realize that I'm emotionally healthier than I thought I was."

Cherry grinned. "Always nice to feel superior, isn't it?"

Evelyn said, "Will somebody go along with me and Ginger to Adam's funeral? That wasn't anything I'd planned on doing, but I want to be supportive of Ginger, and going to the funeral might help with closure."

Lulu wasn't wild about going anywhere with Ginger, but she knew she wanted to be there for Evelyn. "I'll go, honey," said Lulu. "And I'll get Ben to drive me."

Cherry said, "I'll go, too. Oh, I don't care a fig about Ginger, but I want to be there for you, Evelyn."

Buddy said, "Do y'all mind if I change the subject? Too much dwelling on death at my age gets a little depressing."

"Hear, hear," said Morty. He pointed an arthritic finger at Peggy Sue, who paused while applying lipstick. "Weren't you telling me something nice about your granddaughter and Derrick? I do love the young people."

"I'd like an update on that situation, too," said Sara. "Derrick is one boy who definitely deserves a fun date."

Peggy Sue put the lipstick back in her purse and leaned forward. "Yes, honey, they are going *out*! And Peaches is just *thrilled*."

Lulu shifted a little uncomfortably on her wooden chair. "Have they talked, then? Did Peaches call him up?"

"She's giving him a buzz after school this afternoon." Peggy Sue lifted up a plump arm to look at her wristwatch. "In a couple of hours, I guess. But Peaches is one determined little cuss, so I can go ahead and promise you that they'll have a date. They're going to go see this cute movie that just came out—*An Evening in Heaven*. It's supposed to be a great date movie." Peggy Sue gave a trilling laugh.

Big Ben said in his booming voice, "I don't know that I've seen Derrick go out on any dates since he's been here."

Lulu shook her head, endangering the loosely wound bun on the top of her head. "No, he hasn't had a single one, as far as I'm aware. I hope the date goes okay, Peggy Sue, I really do. Because I just don't know if the boy will even open his mouth. He can be that shy sometimes."

"I don't think he's all that shy," said Buddy. "I've seen him really open up lately."

"But that's the thing. You don't know which Derrick you're going to see—insecure, shy, quiet Derrick? Or engaged, helpful, smiling Derrick? It makes it hard. I feel sorry for him—he's had such a rough life already and he's just starting out." Sara's eyes looked misty.

Lulu wondered a little about Peggy Sue's grand-daughter. She certainly sounded really outgoing if she was calling up a boy she'd never met in a town she'd just moved to for a date. Was she outgoing? Or was she desperate?

Lulu's worries were interrupted by Flo's sudden appearance. Lines creased her face and she seemed to be in a near panic. Flo said, "I need your help brainstorming, y'all. I'm in desperate straits!"

Chapter

10

There was a general murmuring from everyone that brainstorming would commence.

"You know that crazy bride I've been dealing with?"

Lulu's mind reeled. There had been so *many* crazy brides. Brides who smoked during the ceremony. Brides who ditched their intendeds ten minutes before the ceremony. Brides who had screaming hissy fits with their mamas because they wanted the Spode china pattern, not the Wedgewood. "Um. I'm not sure, Flo. I remember you talking about a crazy bride, but I can't for the life of me think who she was."

Flo waved her still nicely manicured hand around. "Actually, who she is isn't really important. What's important is what's happening to her wedding. She and her mama planned this really la-di-da wedding. It's at the most historic church in Memphis, the reception is at the Peabody, in the Continental Ballroom. Top-notch, you know? Serving prime rib to two hundred and fifty seated guests. Then the bills for that started rolling in— just the bills for the *deposits*, you know? And the bride and her mama were still really gung-ho about their plan. But the daddy? He went absolutely ballistic. Raging, didn't we know that money isn't growing on pine trees out in W. C. Handy Park? His first *house* hadn't cost this much money. . . . Well, you can just imagine."

Morty said, "Those weddings can run into the hundreds of thousands, y'all. It's like these folks want to show off for everybody they know—the finest of *everything.*"

"It sounds like a miserable mess," grimaced Sara. "So what happened then? Since you'd already reserved the reception location, florist, food—"

"And a band," said Flo in a glum voice, swilling her ice around in her tea. "So the crazy bride started off at one end of the spectrum, and now she's dropped all the way to the other end of the spectrum because Daddy was having such a hissy. The bride and her crazy mama are talking about scaling it all the way back to a handful of people and having the reception in their backyard. And they do have a really good-sized backyard, but outdoor weddings scare me to death.

"But then, and I really think this is the mama getting back at the daddy—a little stab here and there, you know? But she and her daughter are really big Elvis fans. *Big* Elvis fans. The father is real stuffy—all business, all the time. He didn't want to drop half a million on the wedding, but he wanted to have a classy event that he can invite his colleagues to. But that's gone out the window. *Now*, Mama and bride are planning to have their wedding at Graceland—you know how they have that wedding chapel in the woods there? And they're inviting two hundred of their very closest friends. And then we're going to go with Elvis's car museum for the reception site. It's right there on the grounds, you know, and they're used to throwing parties there."

Lulu raised her eyebrows. "That's a pretty big change to the game plan. When is this wedding supposed to take place?"

"In a couple of weeks."

"A couple of weeks!? Honey, you're not going to be able to find any entertainment or caterers in that amount of time! I have my calendar booked up for months in advance with all the different bands that play at Aunt Pat's."

A look of pure panic crossed Flo's face. "I know! So what am I going to do? This wedding will be the biggest disaster you've ever seen. And these people will run their mouths to everyone in town until nobody will ever want to hire me again!"

Morty looked at Buddy and Big Ben with a questioning look. They nodded at him and he cleared his throat. "Flo—seeing as how you're a friend and everything—we could possibly step in to play at the reception. The Back Porch Blues Band is at your disposal." He gave a bow.

Flo slumped. "Oh, what a *relief.* I wasn't sure what to do. Are you sure that y'all can squeeze it in? I hate to take advantage of friends."

"Well, now, let's see. I'll double-check my appointment book." Buddy pulled out a tiny calendar from his shirt pocket. "Looks like all I'm doing that day is waving at cars. How about you, Big Ben?"

Big Ben looked thoughtful. "As I recall, I was going to walk around the Costco that day and eat up the free samples they give out. What about you, Morty?"

Morty looked dreamy again and they braced for a tall tale. "There's a pretty lady who mentioned my coming by her house Saturday to sing along with her favorite blues standards. But I think I can reschedule our date."

"Okay, you're booked, then," said Flo, beaming. "But what about the rest of the things—the food and flowers and such?" Flo looked sideways at Lulu.

"Okay, okay, I'm thinking." Lulu rested her chin in her hands and stared into space. Then she slapped the table with her palm. "Got it! This will be a piece of cake. So, you're doing a bit of a campy, Southern wedding, right? Why not just have Aunt Pat's to cater the barbeque and sides? We could bring in a bunch of tea. Somebody else could maybe handle the alcohol."

Now Flo looked excited. "Why not? That would be perfect if y'all could all swing it. I don't think the Bride from Hell is going to refuse—where else are we going to find entertainment and catering at this hour unless I pull in some personal favors?"

"Hold on—Ben's coming out to take a break. Let me ask him real quick so we'll have a better idea."

After Lulu and Flo had explained the problem and possible solution to Ben, he said, "I think that would work out fine, Flo. We'll have to have some help, though. Your party will take place during business hours for Aunt Pat's, so I'm going to need somebody to help out in the kitchen here. And, if you're talking about a couple hundred guests, we're going to have to pull in some extra help to have that work out, too. I can cook the barbeque here at the restaurant, but to serve it we're going to need a lot of hands."

Lulu snapped her fingers. "How about Oliver?"

"Oliver?" asked Flo. "Oliver the murder suspect?"

"Yes, but he's not doing anything but driving Tudy crazy right now. And he's got gobs of restaurant experience. He can help us with both the cooking and serving and other stuff. He'd be perfect! And I know we can rope in Derrick to help out."

Peggy Sue said, "Evelyn and I can do your flowers and Cherry can help out, too! I went to a program at the library a few weeks ago on arranging flowers. I thought maybe I could even get started doing it on the side. There are tons of ways we can set up some pretty greenery, too, to have things look pretty but not cost so much. Cherry, you can help me, right?"

Cherry looked like arranging flowers for a wedding wasn't exactly on her top ten list of things to do on her weekend. But she nodded her head anyway.

Flo said, "Usually my weddings are in big venues so

I've got the staff at the restaurant or hotel helping me out with last-minute details. But if y'all are all coming, I can just get you all to pitch in and help me out!" She gave Lulu, who was closest, a tight hug that made her breath come out in an *umph*.

"I think I'm more looking forward to the funeral than this wedding," muttered Cherry darkly.

It was interesting, decided Lulu, that every movie she'd ever watched featured a gray, dismal, chilly day for funerals. In the heat of the South, the reality was more of a miserable graveside service with uncomfortable-looking mourners with rivulets of perspiration coursing down solemn faces. Every woman her age had on panty-hose, some sort of foundation undergarment, a dress, and heels to show respect for the dead. Old habits die hard and Lulu still wore her usual funeral attire, even though she'd had no respect for this particular deceased.

The Memphis newspaper was there, showing support for their fallen comrade. They were also there because it was a news event to cover—considering Adam's job as Eppie Currian and the fact he was murdered.

There were quite a few other people there, which surprised Lulu. She didn't think Adam would have had so many good connections in Memphis. Particularly considering his enjoyment of blackmailing and "borrowing" money that would probably never be repaid.

A very short, very young minister carefully read the scripture. Lulu looked across the aisle. Ginger was the only mourner who looked genuinely upset. She alternated between sudden hiccups and a silent, shaking crying. Evelyn sat next to her, patting her hand.

When they'd all recited the Lord's Prayer, the service was finally over and the mourners gratefully dispersed. Oliver and Tudy Hatley walked up to Lulu.

Lulu gave Oliver a hug. "I'm surprised to see you here!"

Oliver said grimly, "I just wanted to make sure he's really dead, that's all. There's been some doubt as to that lately."

Tudy walked up to them. "What a miserable day for a funeral! I'm letting y'all know now—if I suddenly kick the bucket, don't make everybody come to a graveside service. Have a church service in the nice, cool, air-conditioned sanctuary. Then y'all can have a nice buffet at our son's house. Dragging folks off to a hot graveside to sweat while a minister drones on sounds real *vengeful* to me."

As Tudy continued extolling the virtues of air-conditioned funeral services, Lulu took a close look at Oliver. His jaw was set. He had some bruising around his eyes and a couple of cuts on his face and hands that Lulu figured must have happened during his fight with Adam. Oliver looked real defensive and Lulu had a feeling that the Memphis police must have already come calling. Considering he'd bad-mouthed the victim all over the Internet, it wouldn't be any wonder.

As if reading her mind, Tudy said, "And the darnedest thing is that the police keep hounding poor Oliver!

They'll show up and ask real politely for him. And Oliver says the same story over and over. I don't understand what they're hoping to get out of it."

A red flush mottled Oliver's neck. He probably wished Tudy would keep quiet. Instead, she kept on fussing about the police, so he stepped in and said, "They're just doing their job, Tudy. And they know I wasn't happy with Adam, once I knew it was him that had ruined the restaurant. They saw all the things I said about him online, remember?"

"Well, but of *course* you exposed him online," said Lulu sympathetically. "After all, he'd made a real mess of your life. It was only natural to try to get him back by damaging his career in return."

"And that's a whole different thing than killing somebody," said Tudy. "I just don't understand why the police don't see it that way."

"Besides," said Oliver, putting his hands up defensively, "I'm not the only person who didn't like the guy." He looked pointedly toward Holden.

Lulu wanted to get over to talk to Holden—and Big Jack, who looked at every gathering as an opportunity to do some stumping. "I did need to ask you something before I forget, Oliver. I have a favor to ask you. You remember Flo, right?" Lulu explained the situation and asked if Oliver could help out at the wedding.

Oliver's face cleared. "Sure, I'd love to help out. I used to do weddings all the time. If you like, I can give you some pointers, too. . . ." He happily prattled for a couple of minutes on the finer points of wedding catering while

Tudy beamed beside him. When he'd wandered off to talk to someone, Tudy gave Lulu a quick hug. "You're a doll. Just look at his face—he actually looks *happy*. I bet he feels like a million bucks right now because someone *needs* him."

"How's it going at the house?" asked Lulu.

"Well, he's not reading the paper to me anymore, but now he's decided to reorganize the kitchen." Tudy made a face. "I think he's planning a coup to take over my kitchen."

"He should know better than that." Lulu clucked. "After all these years? No matter how great he is at cooking in his restaurant, you were always in charge of the kitchen at home. Making all those delectable chicken pot pies," she said, feeling a hungry twinge in her stomach.

"I know. And I told him that I wasn't going to cook in a kitchen where I didn't know where everything was. And then he told me that was just fine with him!" Tudy's outrage bubbled through her voice.

"Don't worry," said Lulu. "We'll think of something to keep him busy. If I hear of anyone looking for a restaurant manager, I'll give you a buzz." Lulu saw a troubled frown pass across Tudy's face. "Is there anything else bothering you, honey? Not that having an unemployed husband isn't enough."

Tudy blinked hard a few times. "It's really not anything. Like I told you earlier, Oliver told the police the same story over and over again. The truth is the *truth*! It's just that . . . well, I know how upset Oliver was about

Adam. He blamed that man for all our troubles. The day that Adam died, though, something funny happened. He came back from lunch all beat-up looking. You saw him! When I asked him what had happened to him, he was real evasive. Said something about tripping up somewhere and skinning himself. But you don't get those kinds of cuts and bruises from falling down, do you? Not on your face."

Oliver probably hid the truth from Tudy because she couldn't keep a secret to save her soul, thought Lulu. And Lulu didn't feel right telling Tudy what Big Jack had told her. . . . There wasn't really a good way to say it without dragging his name and his problems into the story, too. Instead, she said, "Tudy, I wouldn't worry my head about it, sweetie. He probably just didn't watch where he was going and took a tumble, just like he said."

"I hope," muttered Tudy. But she didn't look convinced.

Holden Parsons was the next person Lulu wanted to talk to. After hearing about the baked bean incident, she wondered if still waters ran deep. He didn't exactly fit Lulu's mental image of a murderer, though. He was an older man wearing a suit that was just a little too big for him, as if he'd lost some weight after his restaurant-reviewing days ended. His thin white hair on his balding head was combed back severely and his hands made nervous, fluttering gestures when he talked.

And right now he looked fairly animated as he talked to some men who seemed to be from the Memphis newspaper. Lulu moved a little closer and heard Holden say, "So, as I was saying, since you don't have a critic anymore, I wanted to let you know that I was available to come back to the office if you needed me to." The words came out in a rush.

The tall newspaper man hesitated and looked over at his colleague. "Well . . . to be honest, we haven't really decided what we want to do with that spot yet. Plus, we sort of transitioned into a new direction with the *Memphis Journal* and we liked the modern approach he took and the readers he brought to the paper. We might want to continue on that trajectory."

Holden's voice rose to a higher pitch. "Remember how you always liked what I wrote? Remember the piece I did on that Italian restaurant? You said it really cracked you up. I can *change* my writing voice, y'all. I can write however you want me to."

The two men shared a look again. "We know you can," said the shorter one. "But the fact is that everybody knows who you are. Adam was able to visit these restaurants under the radar and get the scoop without anybody knowing who he was."

"I could disguise myself!" said Holden. "I could change my clothes, put on a wig. No one would know it was me!"

Lulu thought that the taller man was looking bored. "Look, Holden," he said. "You've let us know that you're available. We get it. Now, if you don't mind, just leave the ball in our court. We'll call you up if we need you."

"All right," said Holden reluctantly. "You still have my telephone number?"

"Sure. We've still got it."

"Just in case, here's my card." And Holden pulled out an old wallet, sifted quickly through it, and picked out a card, which he handed over with dignity.

The shorter man took it and nodded. But Lulu could tell that the card was going to be dumped right into the circular file as soon as Holden wasn't watching. Poor Holden, thought Lulu. He clearly represented an older generation of critic to them. They'd been there, done that, and had seen a lot more success from a younger restaurant reviewer. Lulu could see they weren't interested in moving backward. And they were definitely not dawdling on their way to their car.

Holden turned away, saw Lulu, and smiled a greeting at her. Lulu was just opening her mouth when there was a commotion from behind her. She turned to see Ginger Cawthorn, fists clinched and tears streaming down her red cheeks, directing a furious gaze at Holden, Oliver, Big Jack, and Ben. Evelyn stood beside her, making hushing noises in an unsuccessful attempt to calm Ginger down and get her out of the cemetery.

11

"I just wanted to tell y'all that I'm not letting this murder go. Adam didn't *have* to die. It wasn't his time yet. Somebody took the best years of his life away from him. The best years of *my* life with him. Don't think you're going to get away with it. I'm going to find you and hunt you down and you'll be sorry you ever thought to lay a finger on him. And don't think I'm not going to find out who killed Adam. Because I've already got some leads, believe me." She stifled another sob.

Everyone around Ginger had frozen. Lulu wished she had some sort of guilt-detection device—but then she noticed that everyone there looked guilty—even Ben. They all listened intently to Ginger with startled looks on their faces. Tudy looked especially riveted and Lulu wondered again how angry Tudy was about Oliver being stuck at home. Evelyn finally succeeded in pulling Ginger away right as she was on the verge of foaming at the mouth.

"Well," said Tudy in a shaken voice. "*That* was really something. And why'd she keep looking at you, Oliver? You're not hiding anything from me, are you?" Her laugh rang hollow.

Oliver said, "Was she looking at me? Who knows—I think this murder has messed with her mind."

"Remind me again," said Ben, "why Evelyn is friends with that woman?"

"Evelyn tells me that they have a bond," said Lulu. "Evelyn says she's trying to do some healing and Ginger is helping her do that."

"It sounds like Ginger thinks that the *murderer* was the one who wronged her," said Oliver, looking like he had a bad taste in his mouth. "You'd think Ginger would have some pride and just move on." He stopped talking abruptly as his phone buzzed to let him know he'd gotten a text. He frowned at the device as if he'd never seen it before.

Big Jack laughed, but it wasn't the natural sound that it usually was. "Funerals are usually all about closure," he said. "But it sounded to me like she was doing some opening instead of closing."

Ben was looking curiously at Big Jack. "I'm surprised that you came. I didn't even realize that you knew Adam."

Big Jack briefly glanced over at Lulu, saw in her eyes that she hadn't mentioned anything to Ben about Big Jack's problems with Adam, and said, "Ben—you know

I know *everybody*." He glanced at his watch. "Good thing this funeral is over because I'm absolutely starving. I was worried my stomach was going to start growling at me during that preacher's longwinded prayer."

Lulu said, "Want to come back to the restaurant with us? We'll give you our special friend price."

"Wish I could, Lulu, but I've got to go meet with my accountant and he's outside Memphis. I'll have to grab something on my way out of town." He looked mournful. "And all this fast food is making me a bigger Big Jack than usual."

Lulu frowned. "Where did Ben go? I tell you, I can't keep track of that boy. Shoot—looks like he's over at the car, waiting on me. See you later, Big Jack."

On the way to the car, Lulu caught up with Holden, still milling around the cemetery. "I'm actually doing a little looking around—for Evelyn, mainly," said Lulu. "She felt like she was one of the main suspects because of her involvement with Adam. I'm just trying to help her clear things up."

Holden looked wilted. Even his bow tie drooped. "Well, that's really nice of you, Lulu. I'm sure Evelyn appreciates your friendship."

"We're friends, too, Holden. Think of all those years that you worked for the newspaper and came in to visit with us. You always wrote either nice things about restaurants, or wrote really constructive criticism of places you thought needed improvement." Lulu smiled gently at Holden.

His thin lips trembled a little. "Yes, that's true. I always did my best, even if it wasn't always recognized or appreciated by the paper."

"And I know," said Lulu, reaching over and squeezing Holden's cold hand, "how hard it hit you when you lost your job at the newspaper. I know it hurt when you'd invested so many years into doing a good job for them and then you're replaced by someone new . . . and younger."

Holden winced and nodded.

"My question has to do with something that Ben noticed the day Adam was murdered. He said that he'd gone bulldozing up to you and told you about Eppie Currian's real identity. He said . . . well, he said you were shopping for baked beans."

Holden's face turned even paler and now drops of perspiration appeared on his upper lip.

"And I think you probably know," said Lulu in a gentle voice, "that Adam's body was found covered with baked beans."

"I do know that," said Holden, clearing his throat. His voice was still very dry. "Yes. Let me tell you what happened, Lulu. It's not what you think."

Holden took a white handkerchief from his jacket pocket and dabbed at his mouth.

"You're right—Ben did see me in the grocery store and tell me about Adam being the food critic. And I was holding a can of baked beans. The *reason* I was holding a can of baked beans"—and Lulu wanted to give him a reassuring hug when she saw how stiff he stood as he tried to hold in his emotions—"is because after I lost my job with the paper, I also lost all my income. And, unfortunately, I've never been much of a saver. So when Adam took over my job, he lost me my total livelihood and means of support.

"I've been boiling mad, ready to erupt, for weeks now. It's terrible to go from nice meals in nice restaurants to baked beans and baked potatoes at home. So when Ben told me this, all I could really hear was my heart pounding because I was so furious. I even knew exactly where the guy lived—he was in my same condominium building.

"At first I was just planning to go home, eat my early lunch, and maybe think of a way to talk to this Adam about it. I don't know exactly what I thought I'd gain by talking to him! It wasn't like he was going to apologize and tell me I could have my old job back. But I suppose I wanted to just let him know what he'd cost me by angling for my job.

"So I went home and heated up the beans on the stove. And then I looked out the window and saw Adam—standing right near the river, smoking. Just seeing him made me so livid that I saw red. All thought of serious discourse or any reproachful lectures flew out the window and the next thing I know I'm marching down the stairs with a bowl of baked beans in my hands."

"Did you see anybody on your way down?" asked Lulu, thinking of Evelyn.

Holden shook his head. "But I'm not even sure I'd have noticed if I had. I was that focused. I walked right down the path, down to the river, called his name, he turned around, and I flung the beans right at his expensive suit. He had baked beans all over it." Even now, Holden's voice sounded triumphant.

"Did he say anything?" asked Lulu.

"Nothing I can repeat in nice company," said Holden, with a rather prissy pursing of his lips. "But I did notice that he looked awful, even before I threw the beans all over him. It looked like he'd been in a fight or something—he was all banged up. And the suit looked like it had dirt on it, which was very odd since it was an expensive suit."

That would be resulting from Oliver's push down the stairs, thought Lulu.

"Has Ben . . . said anything to the police?" asked Holden, anxiously twisting his handkerchief in his hands. "I promise that's all that happened. I stomped right off after saying something like, 'That's what you get for stealing people's jobs.' He was very much alive when I left him."

"No," said Lulu, squeezing Holden's hand again. "No, he didn't say anything to the police. I think he was hoping you had an explanation like the one you just gave me."

He looked over toward the gravesite and said, "When I heard Adam was dead, it made me happier than anything had in months."

"What was all that about?" asked Ben as he drove her back to the restaurant. "Having a heart-to-heart with Holden?"

"Just confirming that you were right about those baked beans. He threw them, all right. But he didn't kill Adam—just saw the opportunity to ruin his fancy clothes, is all."

Ben looked glum. "Doesn't sound like a very likely story, Mother. Now I'm thinking that I've incited somebody to murder. That couldn't be a very good thing to have in St. Peter's book when I'm standing at the Golden Gate."

"Pooh! Holden wouldn't hurt a fly. He's practically helpless." But inside Lulu wasn't really so sure.

Derrick was waiting for Lulu on the front porch of Aunt Pat's when they got back to the restaurant. Ben reached out and ruffled Derrick's long hair as he walked by on his way back to the kitchen. "Remember, Derrick, the invitation is open to you to go hunting with me this weekend. We could go out, take the dogs with us, enjoy nature, and break away from all the ladies here at Aunt Pat's who are forever nagging at us." He gave a wicked look at Lulu.

"It's more like you'll go out there and eliminate nature," said Lulu, sitting down in the high-backed wooden rocker. "And I don't know exactly what kind of help Babette would be to you out in the field." Lulu looked innocently at Ben.

He colored a little. "I wasn't talking about taking Babette out hunting. I'd take the Labs, of course. Babette might get hurt."

Babette was the ratlike, yippy dog that Coco and Ben adored. It hated Lulu with a passion and followed her around, baring its teeth.

"Oh, I don't know. She might be good at flushing doves out," said Lulu mildly.

But when Ben looked hard at her and saw the traces of a smile pulling at the corners of her mouth, he said darkly, "No one really *understands* Babette."

"Besides, the ladies you're talking about wanting to escape are the very ones who help keep you straight; you should know that by now. I shudder to think what kinds of outfits you'd be wearing if you didn't have Sara pick out your clothes for you every day."

Ben looked offended. "She doesn't put them out for me in the mornings, Mother. I don't know what you're talking about."

"She may not lay them out for you, but she'll send you right on back to the closet if you've got a tacky combination on, won't she?"

Ben looked vexed.

"That's what I thought," said Lulu, rocking with vigorous satisfaction.

"I'd better get some ribs going," muttered Ben as he walked into the restaurant. He called behind him, "Just remember that the offer stands, Derrick. Anytime you're ready, I'll pull the camo out."

The idea of Derrick in camouflage made Lulu smile. He was a totally modern teenager, dressed in black, baggy clothes. He had long, shaggy hair that he dyed black, a ratty-looking goatee, and had his nose and ear pierced and Lord knows what else. She remembered that he also had a huge tattoo of an eagle on his back, from the rare occasions he took his shirt off. Picturing him dressed up for a hunt was like trying to picture him in a tutu.

Derrick smiled back at Lulu, and she said, "Don't mind Ben. He thinks that *all* teenage boys want to drive out to the middle of nowhere and sit for hours in the heat, humidity, and mosquitoes for a chance to shoot something."

"At least he wants to spend time with me," said Derrick. "It's just not something I'm really excited about doing." His phone buzzed at him from the table, but he ignored it.

"Speaking of something you might not want to do," said Lulu, "did Peggy Sue's granddaughter call you?"

Derrick nodded, and Lulu saw a faint red creeping up his neck. "Yeah. It was kind of weird, Granny Lulu. I'm not used to girls calling me up. Or girls calling anybody up, unless they're dating somebody."

Lulu sighed. "I'm with you on that. It's a whole new, modern world. Peggy Sue knew that you're on the quiet side and for some reason she's really got it stuck in her head that y'all should go out. So she got Peaches to call you, knowing you can be shy." Lulu shook her head. "Times sure have changed."

"Have you found out anything about Peaches?" asked Derrick. It always surprised Lulu that Derrick, with his tough, pierced, tattooed exterior, was so vulnerable. His voice really showed his nerves and told Lulu that he was really worried about the date.

Lulu frowned. "Let's see. Peggy Sue has talked about her from time to time. I think she makes good grades?" Derrick continued looking worried. "And maybe she has a scholarship to a good college in the works?" Lulu didn't seem to be relieving Derrick's mind. "And she doesn't really have any friends because she just moved here."

Derrick was slumping even more than usual and Lulu realized that she hadn't done anything but make the situation worse. A smart girl with no friends. Not the best way to relieve a seventeen-year-old's mind.

"Peggy Sue hasn't been real good about sharing her pictures with me lately, I'm afraid. I remember seeing her school photo about five years ago, but that's not going to help," said Lulu sadly. Five years ago the child had had a mouth full of braces and thick glasses. She'd just keep that little tidbit to herself—a lot could change for a girl in that amount of time. "But Peggy Sue is really cute, you know . . ."

"But she and Peggy Sue aren't related. So Peaches might *not* be cute." said Derrick.

Lulu sighed. "Right. But I'm sure it'll be fine, sweetie." Derrick fiddled with his phone a little.

"What did she sound like on the phone?" asked Lulu.

"Excited," said Derrick in a quiet voice.

Which could either be because she'd never gone out on a date before or because she was just glad to get out of the house. Neither of which was a great thing.

"So you're doing dinner and a movie?" asked Lulu. Derrick nodded. "Well, then, why not have supper

here? At Aunt Pat's? That way, if things aren't going
well with your date, the Graces, Big Ben, Buddy,
Morty—we can all kind of join in and make it easier.
We could make it sort of a group date. You'll be on
your own for the movie, but that part of the evening
isn't so bad—you'll be watching a movie and won't
have to make conversation. What do you think?" She
smiled at him.

Derrick stood up and gave her an unexpected quick
hug. "Thanks, Granny Lulu. I'll text her and let her
know."

Lulu had just finished cleaning up the dining room
and helping get the evening's blues band packed up and
gone. Ben was bleaching the counters when Lulu got a
call on her cell phone.

"Oh, good," said Evelyn. "You're still there. Could
you drop by my house for a glass of wine on your way
home? I feel like I got run over by a Mack truck today—
and then he backed up and ran over me again just to
make sure I was dead."

Evelyn knew well and good that her house was *not* on
the way home to Lulu's—which just proved to Lulu how
badly Evelyn needed somebody to talk to.

"Of course, sweetie! Be there in a jiff."

Evelyn was already in a fluffy pink robe over silk
pajamas when Lulu got there. She led the way into her
massive living room, where a bottle of wine and two
glasses sat on an antique mahogany table. "I really ap-

preciate your coming by today, Lulu. Today has been an epic disaster from start to finish and you've been a sweet friend to share it with me: going to that awful funeral; coming by here after you've had a long afternoon on your feet at the restaurant." She shook her head. "What a great friend you are. And believe me—Tommie appreciates it. I was going to force her to stay here and talk to me after she was supposed to go home if I didn't have someone to cry to."

"Well, of course I was coming by! I'd like to see somebody stop me. What on earth happened this afternoon?"

But Lulu had an inkling of what it might be, so she wasn't totally surprised when Evelyn said, "The police questioned me all afternoon. And they were there at Adam's funeral, too—did you see them? They think I killed Adam."

"Evelyn, I think it's pretty standard for some member of the police department to attend the funeral of a murdered person when they're in the middle of the investigation. Besides, they could have been there looking at Holden, Ginger, Oliver, Big Jack—or even Ben. You don't know that they're wanting to pin the murder on *you*."

The wine chugged as it splashed into the wineglasses under Evelyn's heavy hand. "I don't know it, no. But they sure wanted me to believe it this afternoon. I tell you, Lulu, they really made me feel like I was in a pickle.

"They said, 'So, Mrs. Wade, you were actually *in* the

deceased's condominium, wrecking it and recording a malicious phone message around the time that he was murdered. Is that correct?' And I said, 'Well, yes. But y'all have to credit me with more intelligence than that. If I'd murdered him, then I sure wouldn't have wanted to point the investigators' attention in my direction.'"

"What did they say to that?" asked Lulu, thinking that Evelyn had made a pretty good point.

"Unfortunately, they started in on the physical evidence they'd found that I'd been at the scene of the crime. Remember how I mentioned that I'd gone down near the river and seen Adam's body? That didn't seem to play too well with the police. I mean, they clearly knew that I'd been down there—they found some sort of evidence that tied me to the scene."

Evelyn took a good gulp of the wine, tilting her head back and letting it slide down her throat. "They wanted to know why, if I'd just *discovered* his body and not murdered him, I hadn't called the police."

Lulu had wondered the same thing but figured the shock of finding Adam's body had triggered a flight instinct in Evelyn, who'd always been a little skittish about sticking around. As her high number of ex-husbands could attest to.

"So I told them that of *course* I didn't want to report finding his body. Good Lord! For this very reason, right? I'd just trashed the man's condominium and was clearly furious with him. Why *would* I want to call the police and say, 'Oh, hello. I found the body of this man I loved—and hated. Just wanted to let you know'?"

Lulu said, "Evelyn, I'm positive the police are just trying to figure out if you know anything that's going to help them out. And hard questioning is just the way they go about it."

Evelyn hiccupped. "I won't like prison, Lulu. They have bad food there. And Day-Glo orange jumpsuits. I've gotten used to my massages and mani-pedis. What'll I do?" She took another soothing sip of the chardonnay. "I want to ask you a tremendous favor, Lulu. I'd like you to check into this crime for me."

"Me?" The word came out in a nervous laugh. "Evelyn, what on earth do you mean? I'm a barbeque restaurant owner, not a private investigator."

Evelyn said solemnly, "You're better than a private eye. You're a friend. And you *know* all the people involved in the case. Plus—you care about me. And then there's the fact that you've already solved one murder mystery. Barbeque queen or not—you're a natural."

Lulu looked doubtful.

"Besides," said Evelyn with a disdainful look, "I never want to deal with private investigators again in my life. I've had enough of them during my divorces. I always feel like I'm the one doing something shady."

Lulu said, "Honey, I'll do what I can. I'm not exactly sure what I can find out, but I'll give it a go."

Evelyn continued her glum thoughts. "Because you won't have as much fun during our visits if it's on visiting day at the big house. You'll have to share the visiting room with all kinds of riffraff. And we'll have to talk through one of those germy telephones through a bulletproof panel. And they don't serve chardonnay as refreshments."

Lulu thought for a minute. It was clear that nothing she told Evelyn would do any good. Maybe she was helping her out by just listening to her worry, but she'd rather be helping her feel *better*. She snapped her fingers. "I know! We'll call Pink up."

Evelyn looked at Lulu morosely. "Pink is one of *them*, Lulu. He's not going to do anything to help me out. It's likely he'll come over here and drag me off to jail."

But Lulu was already dialing his number. "I'm ashamed of you, Evelyn Wade! You know Pink is a loyal friend of ours. How many times has he helped us out or given us some information we needed to know?"

Evelyn said, "All right! You're right, Lulu. I'll hear him out. Maybe he can convince me that prison isn't such a rotten place after all."

Pink had pulled in a long shift and was sound asleep when Lulu called. Still, he got up, pulled on some sweats and a baseball cap, and drove over to Evelyn's house. He looked at the emptying bottle of chardonnay and the hiccupping Evelyn with some trepidation.

"Now y'all know I can't do a lot of talking about this case. Hell, it's not even my case! But I can tell you one thing." Pink held his hand out in a traffic cop gesture. "These are the early days of the investigation, okay? We've got to spend some time talking to everybody who *might* have done it."

Evelyn moaned and Pink lifted his hand again. "I said *might* have something to do with it, Evey."

"So Evelyn *isn't* on her way to 201 Poplar, then?" asked Lulu, giving the well-known address for the Memphis jail. "She was getting kind of worried because of the way she'd been questioned at the station."

"Believe me, y'all, as far as I'm aware, there are no plans to put our lovely Evelyn behind bars."

Lulu sat back on Evelyn's damask sofa and released the breath she'd been holding. "Well, now, *isn't* that a relief! That's a relief, *isn't* it, Evelyn?"

Evelyn reached out to a box of tissues that she'd been carrying around with her. She nodded wordlessly, clutching a tissue to her nose.

"There was one thing I was curious to know, though," said Pink, looking at Evelyn intently. "Where were you this afternoon?"

Evelyn made a shooing motion with her hand. "You know where I was, Pink. I was hanging out with your buddies at the police station."

"No, I mean earlier in the afternoon."

Evelyn tossed the tissue at the wastebasket next to her antique secretary. "I was at Adam's funeral—it ended in the early afternoon. Then I left the funeral with Ginger."

Pink's gaze sharpened. "You left the funeral with Ginger Cawthorn?"

"That's right. Why?"

"Ginger Cawthorn was found dead this evening. She was murdered."

Chapter

12

Evelyn turned a pasty white.

Lulu stood up and said, "I think this story can wait a minute, y'all. Let's head into the kitchen. Evelyn, have you even eaten tonight?" Evelyn shook her head. "I'm not sure how Tommie let you get away with that. First things first. Let's get some food and maybe a glass of milk into Evelyn because she's not looking so well."

Although Lulu adored Aunt Pat's kitchen where every pot and pan held a memory, Evelyn's kitchen still gave Lulu a little pang of envy every time she walked in it. The granite countertops and luscious wood cabinets were gorgeous, but what really attracted Lulu was that the kitchen was better equipped than any she'd ever seen, including Aunt Pat's. While Pink and Evelyn sat down at the tableclothed kitchen table encircled by armchair-style chairs, Lulu opened the stainless steel fridge to find something that would stick to Evelyn's ribs.

The perfect fixings for a ham and mushroom omelet were right in front of her. There was even fresh apple wood–smoked bacon to fry and organic milk. Lulu got to work and was soon sliding plates with light, fluffy omelets in front of Pink and Evelyn. Pink took some healthy-sized bites right away while Evelyn toyed at the edges with her fork. After a moment, though, she seemed to realize how hungry she was and tucked into the food.

The food, the milk, the kitchen itself had a lulling effect on the three of them. Pink looked to be drowsing back off to sleep. After Lulu had taken her last bite and made sure that Evelyn had eaten most of her plate, Lulu said, "Now, Pink. Can you tell us a little about Ginger? What happened out there today?"

Pink shrugged. "I'm not sure, Lulu. All I know is that Ginger was discovered by a driver who was walking back to his car in the parking deck. He looked over and noticed she was clearly dead."

Lulu frowned. "What time was she supposed to have been killed?"

"As far as they can tell, it looks like early to mid afternoon."

Evelyn brushed a strand of her chestnut-colored hair from her eyes. "This is all simply unbelievable. I was there with her at the funeral today. Then we went to lunch together. She was just as alive as anybody!" she said defensively.

Pink sighed. "Well, honey, of *course* she was! She *was* alive then. I'm sorry," he said, holding his hands up. "I know she was your friend."

Evelyn hesitated. "I don't know if 'friend' is exactly the right word. We were *trying* to become friends. But we had different ways of looking at things."

"Like what?" asked Pink.

Evelyn looked at Lulu for help, and Lulu said, "Like the way Evelyn thought Adam was scum and the way Ginger was trying to keep his memory alive and find his killer. And the fact that she told *everybody* at the funeral that she had some information about the murder and would find out who did it is probably what got her killed to begin with."

"That could be," said Pink, mulling it over. "I did want to hear some more about the lunch that Evelyn and Ginger had, though. Could you tell me a little about it?"

Evelyn sat very still and looked very small in her fluffy robe. "Well . . . we went to Dyer's. And we had burgers, both of us. I had some chili cheese fries. I got a little chili and cheese on my dress, actually."

Lulu made clucking noises and said, "You can probably get it out if you spray it and wash it with a little Biz. You wouldn't believe some of the stains you can get out."

Pink moved restlessly. "That does sound like a right nice lunch, Evelyn. But I was thinking more about what might have happened *during* your lunch. Or what might have been said."

Evelyn sat silently.

"Because somebody did come forward, Evelyn, and described a woman who matches your description, having an argument with Ginger outside Dyer's."

"How could they be sure it was me?" said Evelyn. She didn't sound exactly sullen, thought Lulu, but she sure didn't seem excited about offering up any information.

"Well, they didn't *exactly* know who you were, but the description was a woman with reddish hair, huge Chanel sunglasses, and a designer outfit. I'm thinking you fit that profile pretty well. And you just told me you went to Dyer's with Ginger."

Now Evelyn frowned crossly. "All right. Yes, we had an argument. It started inside the restaurant. Ginger was just being so *foolish*. She seemed to think that we needed to build some kind of shrine to Adam instead of closing that chapter on our lives. I told her she needed to move on—to get a life. I was trying to be *nice*. I wanted to try to find her somebody else to go out with . . . a good man. Someone who wouldn't cheat on her with lots of other women. She was just being so headstrong."

And Lulu knew that Evelyn wasn't somebody easily crossed. If she wanted to help you, you by golly let yourself be helped. And you thanked her for it.

"So her being headstrong made you mad," said Pink.

"Shoot yeah, it made me mad!" said Evelyn. "She was going to hold on to the memory of someone who wasn't worth the time. Her mindset made me furious." She was gritting her teeth even now. "But not mad enough to shoot her."

Pink raised his eyebrows. "I didn't tell you she'd been shot. How'd you know that little tidbit?"

Evelyn waved her ringed hand around. "Because Adam was shot! How else?" She didn't look Pink in the eye.

Lulu said, "This all happened at a deck off Beale Street? Wouldn't somebody have heard the shot? That's during the lunch crowd—the whole world would be outside that time of day."

Pink shrugged. "If you think about it, Lulu, Beale Street is a pretty noisy place. You've got blues bands playing. Hawkers are standing outside, hollering at people to come in and try the restaurant's daily special. There's even that construction going on one street over and it's almost impossible to hear over a pneumatic drill. And if you're in a restaurant, they're all full of people running their mouths, and plates and glasses clinking. It's not like it was an explosion or something. Same with the shot that took Adam out—it's just not something that called attention to itself."

"What I'm not sure about," said Lulu, "is why someone would want to kill Ginger. I completely understood how Adam might end up dead—he had this talent for pushing people out of their jobs or making them furious at him. The only thing I can think as a motive to murder Ginger is that she was telling everyone at the funeral that she had a lead to the killer."

Pink said, "Well, right now it's all speculation because we really *don't* know. And you're right, Ginger might have had some information that the murderer was worried she'd share with the police. We've also found, in our investigating, that Adam and Ginger had a joint business venture going on."

Evelyn frowned in confusion. "What—like they were business partners, not only marriage partners?"

"Business partners, but not in a normal business. They were in the blackmailing gig together."

Lulu said, "They were blackmailing people together? One of them would provide information and the other would be the heavy?"

"We're not sure exactly how they set it up, but information we found in Ginger's house definitely pointed to the fact that they were in it together."

Evelyn looked irritated. "How does a blackmailing business work, anyway? You can't exactly hang out your shingle and tell everybody what you do. How do you drum up customers?"

Pink laughed. "I think it probably just takes a couple of customers to make it worthwhile. It's not like you have to have office space or advertising. Any money you make is just icing on the cake. As long as you don't end up getting arrested—or killed."

It was after two o'clock when Lulu finally made it back home and climbed under her floral comforter to fall into a hard sleep. When the alarm went off at seven o' clock, she groaned and burrowed deeper under the covers. The day itself wasn't even conducive to getting up—rain splattered down on her roof and dripped down her old windowpanes. She finally dragged herself out from the warm sheets and off to shower and dress.

Breakfast seemed really unappetizing to her in her present state of grogginess. Lulu was usually one for a real country breakfast to sustain her through the day— scrambled eggs, sausage patties, fluffy biscuits, grits, and fresh-squeezed orange juice. Seeing as how she'd *had* breakfast at Evelyn's, she just didn't feel like it again. Instead she poured a tub of vanilla yogurt into her blender along with some frozen fruit, some orange juice, and a little bit of cereal, blended it smooth, and took it with her to drink on the go.

She'd just gotten to the restaurant when her cell phone started singing "Zip-a-Dee-Doo-Dah" at her. "Lulu? It's Flo. Listen, my batty bride called me up last night at midnight—can you *believe* calling someone up at midnight?—and she wants to have a 'planning summit' she said. With y'all for food and with the Back Porch Blues Band for music. And I guess about the flowers, too, and so I'll have to call the Graces because they were helping me with that. A *summit*? Can you believe it?" Flo sounded completely indignant.

Lulu pulled out a wooden chair and plopped down into it. "Oh no. What time does she want to hold this summit? Because I *did* get a call like that last night and didn't go to bed until after two."

"I'm real sorry about it, Lulu. This woman is plum crazy! Could we maybe talk to her after your lunch rush? Around three o'clock? I'll call everybody and set it up." Flo's voice sounded anxious. This must be some bride.

"Of course we can talk to her then, sweetie. We'll get her all calmed down, don't you worry."

It was amazing how you couldn't really buy class, thought Lulu as she watched Flo's "batty bride," controlling mother, and sullen groom. The bride, Ashley, smacked her gum with at a rhythmic pace and interrupted her mother, Cynthia, at every opportunity. The groom, whose name Lulu hadn't caught—if it'd even been tossed to her—looked like he'd rather be anywhere else.

The Graces, Lulu, and the Back Porch Blues Band had all spent the last couple of hours trying to calm down the wedding party. Aunt Pat's handled large crowds every day. Big Ben, Buddy, and Morty had played for big crowds in their day. And the Graces could put some mean bouquets and arrangements together, even in a pinch.

"We need everything to be *perfect*," said Cynthia. "We'd planned on this being the social event of the year, you know. Now we've ended up downsizing it and adding an element of *fun*." Lulu guessed that having the wedding at Graceland and having barbeque on the reception menu was the "fun." "But we can't compromise our goal of perfection."

Flo took the opportunity to roll her eyes since the

wedding party wasn't looking in her direction. "Believe me, Cynthia, this wedding couldn't be in better hands. This is going to be a wedding that people are going to be talking about for a long, long time."

Ben had come out of the kitchen for the meeting and was already thinking about the financial end of things. "I know we're going to be making a lot of barbeque for the reception and I just wanted to make sure that everything was sound, financially. I know that cutting back was the reason you decided to go this route to begin with."

Cynthia and Ashley looked at each other, then Ashley looked down at the nail she was picking apart. "You'll be paid, don't worry about that."

"Ashley," persisted Flo, looking across at the blond bride, "you've squared everything with your dad, haven't you?"

Ashley snorted. "Daddy has been horrid. He didn't want to cough up the money for the Peabody wedding and now he's just as upset about the Graceland one. He doesn't want anything to do with it." Her lips poofed out in an unattractive pout. The groom looked worried.

"It doesn't matter," said Cynthia, carefully straightening the red checkered tablecloth with hands sporting huge diamonds. "I'll pay for this myself, so you don't have to worry about your money."

Big Ben said, "I'm just glad to know that I shouldn't announce a father-daughter dance when we're playing the reception. That could have been reeeal awkward."

"Who's giving you away?" asked Flo, knitting her

brows. "I thought your dad was going to walk you down the aisle."

"My first cousin will walk with Ashley," said Cynthia in a bored voice. "You probably know him—Big Jack Bratcher. Doesn't he come here for barbeque just about every week? He was the one who said it was fine to bring you on board—that you'd do a good job."

Lulu didn't know whether she should feel gratitude to Big Jack or fuss at him for getting her involved with his impossible family.

Cynthia drew in a deep breath. "Oh my God. I forgot about the photographer. Have you gotten us a photographer? We have *got* to have a photographer."

Flo rubbed the sides of her face as if her head hurt. "Cynthia, as I already mentioned to you, all the photographers I know are booked up. They have *other weddings* to do on Ashley's wedding day. They can't just drop what they're doing."

Cynthia's right eye started twitching. "I don't see why they can't just fit a couple of extra hours into their day."

"But it's *more* than just a couple of hours, Cynthia. You've got to do portraits of the bride, bride and groom, parents of the bride and groom—the whole shebang. *And* pictures of the bride getting ready for the wedding. *And* the actual ceremony *and* the reception *and* the bride and groom running through the birdseed to their getaway car. It's *lots* of *hours*." Flo looked like she was about to cry. Lulu, like any respectable older lady, pulled out a perfectly folded fresh tissue from her sleeve and handed it to Flo in case she needed it.

Peggy Sue was goggle-eyed. "Y'all didn't get a photographer first thing? I know brides who booked the photographer before they even booked the groom! You have to look good for the portrait that runs in the paper, you know? And those wedding pictures live forever, so you have to find somebody who knows all the tricks. I thought y'all would have done that before anything."

Flo talked between her gritted teeth. "Yes, well, we *did* that, Peggy Sue. I've planned a few weddings, you know. But when Cynthia asked me to try to renegotiate the contract with Shaun Westerfield, he didn't take it so well."

Cynthia gave a short laugh. "He's obviously completely in love with himself. Thinks he's some sort of artist whose genius would be compromised by taking a penny less."

"Well, and that may be, but I warned you about him when you asked me to reserve him at the very beginning. You get some really amazing pictures from him, but you have to put up with all his nonsense, too. But now he's dropped us and gone off in a snit and we can't find anybody else on such short notice."

There was a small but insistent cough behind Lulu and she turned to see Holden Parsons standing there, looking earnest. "If I could say something," said Holden in his trademark hesitant way. "I wondered if I might be able to help you out with the photography. Since you're in a pinch." His fingers fumbled as he reached for a chair to pull up.

"And who," said Ashley, a Cynthia-in-training, "are *you*?"

"Forgive me for not introducing myself first. I'm Holden Parsons and I used to work for the *Memphis Journal*."

"As a photographer?" asked Cynthia, perking up a little.

"No. No, actually, as a restaurant critic. But I had to take my own photos of the restaurant and different dishes for the paper. So I became very good. And the pictures ran every week."

Ashley slumped a little and looked like she'd lost interest. "Oh. So it was just food. Well, that would work for pictures of the cake maybe. But I'm not made of flour or eggs."

And certainly no sugar of any kind, thought Lulu as Cynthia snorted a laugh.

Holden, always so reticent, had turned pink at his ears and was already mumbling some excuses, fingering his drooping bow tie, and making motions to leave. Lulu stopped him.

"Now hold on a minute, y'all. This doesn't make a lick of sense. I believe in something we call serendipity. And what I'm seeing here is someone who used to do some photography for a major newspaper and is currently unemployed. And I'm also seeing someone who is throwing a wedding that they don't have a photographer for and have no hope of *getting* a photographer for. This seems like a match made in heaven to me."

Flo said briskly, "Count on Lulu to make sense! Tell you what, Holden. Do you have any kind of a portfolio of your articles and pictures?"

Holden looked abashed. "Nooo . . . well, not really. At the time it just didn't seem important."

Cynthia and Ashley rolled their eyes.

"Okay, well how about if you *took* some pictures. Maybe go out and pretend you're on assignment or something? Take some and then put them in a folder and we can show Cynthia and Ashley . . . and . . . um, Peter, of course." Flo made a vague gesture across the table.

Lulu guessed that Peter was the silent groom.

Holden smiled eagerly. "I could do that!"

Lulu snapped her fingers. "Not only that, but while you're out snapping pictures, Holden, you could take some for Aunt Pat's. Derrick told me the other day that the website and blog needed some more pictures. He's using a lot of clip art, he said, and he thought it would look a lot better with some photos from inside and out-side the restaurant."

"You could take pictures of the Back Porch Blues Band playing," said Morty. "That would look cool to the tourists and might even help us to book some gigs."

"And maybe even take some shots around downtown Memphis." said Lulu. "It'll look good on the website and might mean that tourists who are planning a trip to Memphis could put Aunt Pat's on their itinerary."

Cynthia and Ashley were losing interest again. Ash-ley blew a large bubble with her gum and her mother said, "Just make sure we see them first. We don't want just anybody taking pictures at the wedding, you know. We want this wedding to be *good*."

"It's going to be perfect," said Flo, who sounded like she was using the words as a mantra. "Perfect!"

After Cynthia, Ashley, and Peter left, Ben hurried back to the kitchen to start cooking for the supper rush and the others all slumped back in their seats. "That was painful," said Buddy. "If you weren't such a great friend, Flo, I'd be telling you there was no way I could deal with those women."

"I'm so sorry, y'all! I promise you that I'll never drag you into something like this again. Y'all are the *best*— you're really saving my life."

"Did you know that Big Jack was Cynthia's cousin?" asked Lulu curiously.

"Nope! But I'm not really surprised. Big Jack is *everybody's* cousin."

"So then I guess Oliver is related to them, too? He's Big Jack's cousin, too."

"Probably somehow. It'll be an interesting wedding."

"On to more interesting topics," said Peggy Sue, leaning eagerly over the table at Lulu. "Is Derrick just thrilled about his date with Peaches tonight?"

Lulu could think of several adjectives, but "thrilled" unfortunately wasn't among them. He was more worried and nervous than anything else. "It should be a fun night for them," she said brightly, not addressing the question head-on.

"I thought it was so sweet of Derrick to suggest they have their supper here at Aunt Pat's before they go to the movie! It just shows how excited he is—he wanted to introduce Peaches to a place that's really important to him and his family. It just chokes me up." And Peggy Sue did just that, to Lulu's alarm. Her little round glasses fogged up with the sudden cloudburst and she took them off and rubbed them with a tissue. Lulu had no idea that Derrick's suggestion might be taken that way.

"Well, and I also thought it might be easier, you know? Easier for the children. First dates are always pretty hard, you know, and they're awfully young. Derrick really doesn't have much experience dating yet."

Peggy Sue said, "Oh! We could all be around in the restaurant when they have their date! I'm just dying to see the two of them together—I think they'll be the cutest things. When are they meeting for supper? Can we just stay on?" She looked at her watch.

"I think they made it for six o'clock, Peggy Sue. They were going to try to catch the seven thirty movie since they have school tomorrow."

"Perfect! It's already five fifteen since that summit took the better part of forever."

Flo winced.

"Now, Flo, it's not your fault that those people are tacky. And now we're here just forty-five minutes before their date! I'm settling in for the long haul." A waitress checked in at the table and Peggy Sue said, "Could you bring me a drink, love? Heck, bring everybody at the table a drink! We need one after that meeting."

When Lulu excused herself from the group to check on things in the kitchen, Sara scurried up to her. "You should see Derrick!" she said with a big grin on her face.

"Is he a nervous wreck?" asked Lulu with a worried frown.

"I think he probably is, but he's hiding it pretty well. He just came in through the back door a few minutes ago. The whole time since he's been back from school, he's been getting ready for tonight at the house. And he looks great!" Sara's freckled face beamed.

"He's not wearing all black?" asked Lulu. "He's brushed his hair?"

"He's wearing a *golf shirt* and regular *blue jeans*!"

Lulu's eyes widened. "This I've got to see for myself."

She walked through a short hall to the office, where, sure enough, Derrick sat watching cartoons with Ella Beth and Coco. And he looked, thought Lulu with satisfaction, *wonderful* all cleaned up.

Derrick looked up and smiled at Lulu. She said, "Hi, sweetie! You look like a million dollars. Are you all set for tonight?"

Derrick took a deep breath. "I'm as ready as I'll ever be."

Lulu cleared her throat a little. "I—um—I did want to tell you that Peggy Sue is going to be one of the gang in the dining room during your date. I know that might not be really ideal, but . . ."

Derrick shrugged. "Granny Lulu, it's no big deal. If the date isn't good, I need all the help I can get. Peggy Sue can talk to anybody about anything, so at least

Peaches and I won't be just staring at each other." He frowned and a worried look crossed his features again. "I wish I knew what I was getting into—if she's a cute girl or if she's fun, or what."

Lulu leaned over and patted him on the back. "Well, honey, she's going to be here real soon, so you won't have too much longer to worry about that. And maybe recommend the Brunswick stew to her tonight on the side. Your Uncle Ben has whipped up an amazing batch today."

Derrick's attention was pulled back to the cartoons (which seemed to be featuring a lot of explosions). Lulu felt something tickling her hand and looked down. Ella Beth was under a table, putting a small scrap of paper in her hand with one hand and holding a finger to her lips with the other.

Lulu said, "Okay, honey, well, I'll see y'all in a little bit," and she walked out to the hall.

The scrap of paper said "Meet me in the ladies' room for an update." Lulu frowned at it before remembering that Ella Beth had vowed she would investigate Adam's death since she'd discovered his body. A very serious-looking Ella Beth met her in the restroom.

"Remember how I've been investigating the case?" she asked in a brisk, professional voice. "Well, I've been doing some hiding out, let me tell you. I've been under tables and lurking behind the rocking chairs, and hiding just around the corner of Aunt Pat's outside. Collecting data, you know."

Part of Lulu wanted to smile, but she didn't dare. Ella

Beth was one tough nine-year-old. Besides, it wasn't really a laughing matter. What if she were caught when someone really *was* saying something they didn't want anyone else to hear? "But I told you to be really careful, Ella Beth. Remember? I told you that there was somebody dangerous out there."

Ella Beth beamed. "And that's what I was! I was *very* careful. I was so sneaky, Granny Lulu. Nobody even knew I was there—not even you! Because you didn't know anything about this until I just said something!"

Point taken. "All right, sweetie. Tell me what it was that you found out."

Chapter

13

"It was a couple of days ago that I heard it. You've been busy," said Ella Beth with a reproachful look at Lulu, "so I haven't even gotten a chance to tell you about it. Remember that day Aunty Evelyn came in with that other lady? What's her name? With the grayish reddish hair? I was on the porch with B.B. and Elvis, and when I looked through the window into the dining room, it looked like people were really mad."

Lulu knit her brows. "Her name was Mrs. Cawthorn. Now how could you tell that people looked mad all the way from the porch, Ella Beth?" Really, the child was just too observant. And Lulu was still irritated with her for nosing around in something that could hurt her.

"Oh, it's *easy*, Granny Lulu! You could tell the grown-ups were upset. Aunty Cherry's face was almost purple. Big Ben had that look on his face like something smelled rotten. And the woman with the red hair was holding her hands in fists.

"A minute later, Aunty Evelyn and the red-haired lady were talking together, so I hid behind one of the picnic tables. Grown-ups never see anything down low," she said in a matter-of-fact voice.

Lulu had to agree with that. "Or up high, either," she said.

"Miz Cawthorn's cell phone rang and Aunty Evelyn said she'd call the other lady later and she left. But the red-haired lady sat down on the porch and started talking to the person on the phone. Adam was her *angel*. Adam was *such* a wonderful and special person. She was just so upset that Adam was dead. Her life was *over!*" Ella Beth rolled her eyes. "I felt bad that the man was dead. Really bad. Especially since I found him. But this lady was all gushy about it. It just sounded kind of fake."

Lulu considered this. She hadn't really thought about it, but Ginger's expressions of grief really did seem over the top. Had she been playing it up a little? She really wasn't all that upset, but she was just trying to grab the spotlight and get everyone to feel sorry for her?

"And then, while she was still talking about Mr. Wonderful Adam, Mr. Parsons came onto the porch."

Lulu vaguely remembered Holden being at the restaurant that day. But then, he was there nearly every day since he'd lost his job. He knew everybody at Aunt Pat's, after all, and the food wasn't very expensive. And Lulu had guessed he felt pretty lonely. His wife had died just a couple of years ago and it was probably very quiet at his house. Too quiet.

"And he got *really* mad. Just as mad as the grown-ups in the restaurant. He stood right in front of Ginger on the porch with his arms crossed and his face all red. He even tapped his foot, just like you see in the cartoons. I thought *steam* might start shooting out of his ears, like the cartoons, but it didn't. Miz Cawthorn got off her phone really quick and he started yelling at her right away."

"Yelling at Mrs. Cawthorn?" Lulu tried unsuccessfully to picture this. Holden was such a mild-mannered man with his polka-dotted bow ties; his tidy, unimaginative clothing; and his careful way of talking. But then, she couldn't really see him throwing a can of baked beans at Adam, either.

"He sure was. 'What kind of a crazy lunatic was she?' he said. That one made me smile because he must *really* be mad if Mr. Parsons was saying things like that. Because he knows *all* lunatics are crazy. He said Adam was a leech and a fake and a sneak and, if Miz Cawthorn didn't see that about her own husband, then she must be stupid." Ella Beth's eyes were opened wide, remembering how mad Holden had been.

"What happened then?"

"Miz Cawthorn just looked kind of surprised. Then she laughed at Mr. Parsons and it was a kind of mean laugh. She said that Mr. Parsons didn't know anything *about* Adam. And that Adam had nothing to do with the fact that Mr. Parsons had lost his job. She said it was just something that happened in the marketplace. That maybe if Mr. Parsons had been a better writer to begin with and if his articles hadn't been so boring, then maybe he'd have kept his job at the newspaper.

"Then Mr. Parsons started kind of stuttering. He said that Miz Cawthorn probably didn't even know how to read, so how could she have any idea what his stories were like? It was all Adam's fault.

"Then Miz Cawthorn said, 'You sure are awful mad at him. Maybe you were mad enough to kill him.' And he stomped right off the porch into the restaurant. I figured she was about to go out to the parking lot, but first Evelyn came out for a second. Evelyn asked what Mr. Parsons was so upset about and Miz Cawthorn kind of shrugged. Then she said to Evelyn that she was going to get to the bottom of the murder. She said she knew that somebody went to a meeting with Adam with a gun, prepared to kill him."

Lulu had to wonder what was going through Ginger's head. Of *course* someone came to the meeting with Adam with a gun—he was shot, wasn't he? Lulu gave Ella Beth a hug. "Sometimes grown-ups can get mad and act like little kids themselves . . . but it doesn't mean that Mr. Parsons is going around killing people. And it doesn't mean that Mrs. Cawthorn knew what she was talking about, either. You've told me now— why don't you put it all out of your head and let me worry about it?"

Ella Beth sighed. "Granny Lulu, there's an awful lot in my head right now that everybody keeps telling me to forget. It's easy for them to say it, but hard for me to do it."

Lulu chuckled. "You're right, it's not so easy, is it? But you could try to distract yourself, honey. Why not spend a little extra time with Coco? If you're hanging out with other children, then forgetting will come a little easier to you."

Ella Beth shook her head until her ponytail swung back and forth violently. "Coco just wants to talk about her beauty pageants and what it's going to take to win the Little Miss. Then she starts fussing about Daddy and how he won't let her wear the makeup she needs to be a contender." Ella Beth made a face.

"Now, Ella Beth, you know that's not true! Coco talks about other things, too."

"Yes, ma'am, she does. Like Babette." Lulu saw Ella Beth had a conspiratorial look on her face. She knew well and good that her Granny Lulu was no fan of the yippy, rodent-esque dog that Ben and Coco doted on.

"Well, there's something wrong when you dress a dog up as a cheerleader. Don't you agree with me, honey? I have no idea why that little creature nips at my heels every time I come to your house. B.B. and Elvis just *love* me."

"That's because they're *real* dogs," said Ella Beth fervently. "Babette is a cross between a dog and a squirrel."

The restroom door opened. "Well, *here* you girls are!

Hiding out, hmm? Peaches just got here and she looks like the cutest thing!" said Peggy Sue, bubbling.

"Great! I'll be right there," said Lulu, giving Peggy Sue a smile as she popped right back out the door and off to drag poor Derrick out of the office. She could hear Peggy Sue say, "My camera! I've got to get my camera out," as she hurried off down the hall to the dining room.

Ella Beth said, "Granny Lulu, why do they call them blind dates? Derrick kept calling it a blind date and he was really worried about it."

"A blind date is when you're going into a date blind— you're meeting the person for the first time on the date."

Ella Beth made a face. "So they could be somebody who eats with their mouth open or burps at the table or something?"

Lulu felt a twinge of nervousness for Derrick. "That's exactly right. Come on, Ella Beth, let's go check on Derrick."

"I think I'm going to check on Peaches first. Let him know what he's getting himself into."

Ella Beth opened the door to the dining room and, acting very careless, made a casual loop around the room. She hurried back to the office to report.

"Derrick! It's okay! She's *pretty*! And I don't think she has troll manners or anything, either!"

In fact, thought Lulu, Peaches seemed practically perfect. She gave Derrick a big hug when she greeted him and said, "Gran always knows the best people in the world, so I knew you'd be a great guy!"

She had on a darling outfit, thought Lulu, in a very flattering style for her tall, thin figure. She had long blond hair and sparkling blue eyes. Derrick seemed stricken instead of smitten, though.

It's his nerves! thought Lulu. His old insecurity is rearing its ugly head. Maybe he'd have done better with a really introverted girl or maybe even a less attractive or self-assured one.

But Peaches was quick to try and put him at ease. "I've been looking forward to this like you wouldn't believe," she said. "It's horrible moving to a new town and not knowing a soul. I go a little crazy when I get cooped up inside for too long. Derrick," she said, "you can be my guide for the evening, okay? What's good to eat at Aunt Pat's?"

Peggy Sue chortled and leaned in closer. "I'm dying to hear the answer to this one. Peaches, the boy's *got* to say that everything's wonderful. The owner of the restaurant is right here!"

Derrick looked uncertain, his face red as he stammered, "W-well. It *is* all good." He looked helplessly at Lulu to rescue him, but then remembered, "But the Brunswick stew is supposed to be really great tonight. Maybe you'd like a little bowl of that on the side."

"What kinds of food do you like best?" asked Lulu. "We can get you set up with a barbeque sandwich or ribs. Or you could even have a veggie plate if that's what you usually like."

"I think I like everything," said Peaches, laughing. "I can eat the barbeque and veggies, too."

"Well, Ben whipped up some black-eyed pea salad that's just one of the best things you've ever put in your mouth. It's got this green pepper and red onion in it and the tastes all combine really well."

"Ooh. That sounds delicious! I definitely want some of that."

"Would you like some iced tea?" asked Derrick, shyly. "Lulu makes the best."

"Why thank you, Derrick!" said Lulu, beaming. "I've got two different ones right now, too—a spiced iced tea with orange juice in it, and a regular sweet tea."

And she wondered, as Peaches and Derrick figured out their order, if this date was such a good idea. Would it give Derrick confidence or make him feel even worse about himself? And here he was with a huge audience— Big Ben, Morty, Buddy, and all the Graces.

Plus Oliver, added Lulu as he walked through the door and up to the group. "I thought I'd run by and just make sure we're on the same page with the plans for the wedding—like when we're planning to start cooking that day," he said.

Lulu felt reluctant to leave Derrick, who was still shooting her helpless looks. "Tell you what, Oliver, why don't you run back to the kitchen and talk to Ben while he's cooking. It won't take long for y'all to figure out the plan for the day."

Then, to Lulu's relief, things started going a little better. Derrick smiled a little more and looked more relaxed. Peaches seemed genuinely intrigued by her quiet date and focused on pulling him out of his shell.

Oliver came back out of the kitchen a few minutes later. "Got it all set," he said to Lulu as he pulled up a chair and joined the group. "I just wanted to make sure I knew the plan."

Lulu figured it was more likely that he really didn't have anything else to do except drive Tudy crazy at home. "I figured you two experts wouldn't have a problem getting the wedding plans arranged. Y'all just tell me when to be there and I'll make sure I make it then," she said.

There was a lull in the conversation and Peggy Sue was diametrically opposed to conversational pauses.

"Wasn't it awful about poor Ginger?" She reached out and patted Peaches's hand. "That's why Evelyn isn't here right now. She's that cut up about it. You see, her friend Ginger was murdered yesterday."

Oliver suddenly looked like the breath was knocked out of him. Peggy Sue noticed it and said, "Oh, you didn't know? Yes, it really looks like there's a killer on the rampage—shooting people right and left. It's awful, isn't it?"

Jeanne said, "Oliver, I saw you the other day with Ginger—you were friends with her, too?"

Oliver quickly said, "No, you must be mistaken, Jeanne. Ginger and I weren't friends. We really barely knew each other."

Jeanne's thin face was serious. "But, Oliver, it *was* you. I was driving away from Graceland after my docent duty and I saw you and Ginger talking in a parking lot. I remember it all very clearly because it was so far out—you know how Graceland is a bit of a drive—and because I didn't realize y'all knew each other."

Lulu raised her eyebrows. Jeanne, who read her Bible several times a day, was *not* telling a lie. Of course, she *could* have been mistaken, which was what Oliver clearly wanted her to think.

Peggy Sue's eyes opened wide. "Oh! And did Ginger call you? Because she was asking Evelyn if she had your cell phone number. I think she knew somebody who knew somebody who owned a restaurant or something. So Evelyn gave it to her."

He gave a tight smile. "Maybe she never got around to it before her sudden demise. But, no, Jeanne, it wasn't me you saw. One of the things about being graying, balding, and stout is that you look like every other middle-aged man out there. It's an easy mistake to make. Besides, I had a long dental appointment that afternoon. And, believe me, I'd rather have been hanging out in a parking lot than getting that dental work done." He rubbed his palms against his jeans and Lulu wondered if it was because he was perspiring from nerves.

Jeanne opened her mouth to say something else, but then pressed her lips together tightly. She must have decided not to argue, figured Lulu. Which made sense, because Oliver obviously wasn't going to suddenly admit to being Ginger's mystery man.

"Looks like Evelyn is ready to take on the world again," said Buddy with a nod at the door.

Lulu walked over to greet Evelyn but was beat to it by Big Jack Bratcher, who was just leaving with a to-go box. He gave them both hugs.

"Hi, darlin'," he said to Evelyn. "I wanted to see if you wanted to come to my fund-raising dinner at the lake this weekend."

Evelyn put her hands on her hips, "Didn't I already max out with donations this year? I mean, *really*, Big Jack."

"You sure did—I told you that you were one of my top donors! No, this is just a big thank-you for everything you've done. Everybody *else* has to pay to attend. And, Lulu, why don't you come along with her? You've helped me out a lot by hosting fund-raisers here at Aunt Pat's."

Evelyn was still hemming and hawing. "But we have to schlep three hours out to the lake."

"For crying out loud, Evelyn! You have a mansion sitting right on the water. And one of them fancy salt-water pools. . . . Don't you go there about every weekend? So you and Tommie just pack up, bring Lulu along, and come to my party. I've got that fabulous New South chef—Taylor Franklin—to cook for us. We're going to have some pan-roasted duck. Or, if you want something else, he's also doing a baked grits with some country ham and mushrooms. And his cornbread rivals Lulu's. It's not spicy, though—it's sweet."

Lulu's stomach growled ominously. "Evelyn, let's do it! You could definitely use a break and I could use one, too. I can get away from the restaurant if it's just for a day. Couldn't we head over there early Saturday morning and then come back early on Sunday?"

Evelyn shrugged. "Why not? Except maybe I need to let the Memphis police know where I'm going to be."

Big Jack's eyes widened. "You're not headed out to the pokey, are you, Evelyn? Good Lord. I sure don't need my biggest supporter locked up."

"No! I mean, I guess I'm not. I didn't do *anything*. Well, I didn't do anything but what I've told y'all about—wrecking Adam's condo. But who knows what kind of skullduggery the Memphis police thinks I've been up to."

Big Jack nodded solemnly. "They talked to me, too, Evelyn. But we knew that was coming. Since I left that message on the machine."

"How did it go?" asked Lulu sympathetically. "Were they rough on you with the questioning?"

"Oh sure! Yeah, they want you to think that they *know* you did it. They get you all worked up until you think you *did* do it. They're hoping to get you to slip up or confess or something. But I just told them . . . I'd screwed up and done something stupid. That stupid thing was to cheat on my wife—*not* kill somebody. And I'd been doubly stupid in that I was out in public misbehaving and this twerp took my picture with the lady with his cell phone."

"How did that go over?" asked Lulu.

"Oh, well, they were convinced that I killed him, still. Or at least they acted like they were. But they finally let me go. And so far Lisa doesn't know and I'd *really* like to keep it that way. I've learned my lesson: cheating is for losers. Believe me; I'm not making that same mistake again."

Evelyn covered her mouth, looking like one of those "speak no evil" monkeys. Lulu said, "We won't say a thing about it. And thanks for inviting us to your party. Sounds like fun!"

Chapter

14

The next day, Lulu stood in her closet door and stared at her collection of floral dresses. What kind of occasion was this? She'd hosted Big Jack's fund-raisers before at Aunt Pat's, but they'd always been really casual and fun. They were the kind of events that if a person wore a floral dress they might be *over*dressed for it. She picked up the phone.

"Evelyn? It's me. This fund-raiser for Big Jack—what are you wearing?"

"Oh, Lulu. It's more than a fund-raiser—it's a gala. I read something about it in the paper this morning. It's going to be all glitzy and some folks from the *Memphis Journal* are going to be there taking pictures."

Lulu's heart sank as she looked at her choices. "Well, I have that navy dress. I suppose I could wear that one. Do you remember my navy dress?"

There was a pause on the other end of the line. "Do you mean your funeral dress? The one you pull out for graveside services?"

"Won't that be okay?"

Another pregnant pause. "Tell you what, Lulu. I could use a new gown anyway. Let's go out shopping and find something really fun. Do you mind if I call up Tudy Hatley and see if she can come along? I've been promising myself I'd take her out to do something fun. She's been so bummed out about Oliver and losing the restaurant. And then I saw her when I was grocery shopping yesterday and she looked just *awful*. I guess he really must be driving her nuts or something. We can kill two birds with one stone. Shopping and lunch! A girl's day out! Fun-fun!"

Lulu said, "Okay, Evelyn. As long as y'all can give me some advice about what to buy. I just don't have any idea what to wear to this thing." She hung up and sighed. The word "gown" meant "expensive" in Lulu's book. And shopping, as an activity, rated only slightly lower than cleaning out the refrigerator.

Evelyn squinted at Lulu as she hesitantly walked out of the dressing room. "Now *that* one is a little better. Don't you think that one is better, Tudy?"

Tudy, who'd been very sweet but remarkably unhelpful said, "Lulu, you look *beautiful*!" just like she had the last five times Lulu had shown them a dress.

Lulu looked at herself in the tri-fold mirror and grimaced. "It's cinching my waist and making the fabric poof out in the back. My fanny looks *huge*!" She turned around and looked over her shoulder at herself in the mirror. "It's *not*, is it?"

Both women erupted into soothing noises, "No, of *course* not!" "It's the dress—it's just not the right one."

"That type of fabric gets all bunchy, honey."

Lulu gloomily slouched into the changing room to try on the next dress. "Funny how Evelyn was able to find something right away. Must have something to do with being a size four."

It took three more tries, but finally there was a simple, long black dress that made Lulu feel great when she put it on. With her height (although Lulu was dismayed that she'd been shrinking a little each year), they discovered that she could carry off a longer dress, that black was slimming, and that simple was better. With a huge sigh of relief, Lulu paid for the dress (gulping a little at the price).

As the ladies made their long walk to the food court, Lulu kept looking sideways at Tudy. Something just wasn't right with her. She seemed really distracted and not caught up in Evelyn's conversation about evening bags like she'd ordinarily be.

"Okay, Tudy," said Lulu abruptly. "Spill it."

Tudy knit her brows. "Spill it?"

"What's bothering you, honey? Here Evelyn is having a passionate monologue about beaded evening bags versus sequined evening bags and you're not even jumping in to give an opinion. As girly as you are, you should be telling us all kinds of things about glamorous pocketbooks—where to buy them, what's in style. So tell me—what's on your mind?"

Tudy blinked hard and walked even slower than she had been. "Oh, y'all. I don't know where to start. Oliver is making my life miserable right now!" She sniffed loudly but seemed determined to keep the tears at bay.

"The reading-out-loud thing again?" Evelyn shrugged. "It's annoying, but I think I could overlook it. Or do like Derrick does and just plug yourself into an iPod and nod every once in a while when he's talking to you."

"No," said Lulu. "It's the fact he's trying to reorganize her kitchen right under her nose. That's just something we cooks don't take lightly."

Tudy shook her head violently. "No, y'all. It's even *worse*. Oliver killed Adam Cawthorn. And he was having an affair with Ginger!" This time a dogged tear managed to slip out before Tudy angrily swiped it away. "And he's going to end up spending the rest of his life in the big house!"

Evelyn and Lulu gave each other quick, gawking looks before shutting their mouths and putting an arm around Tudy.

"Now what makes you think such a thing, Tudy? It's hard for me to picture Oliver as a gallivanting murderer," said Lulu.

Tudy gave another sniff. "I told you about the way he looked all beat up that day Adam died. I know he must have gotten in a fight with him. And I was wrong to think it was about the restaurant. I mean—the fact he blamed Adam for putting us out of business was part of it. But now I know the reason that Adam was fighting him . . . because Oliver has been having an affair with Ginger! And Adam was jealous!"

Evelyn winced at her logic. "Whoa. Tudy, I just don't believe a word of this. Remember that Adam and *I* were having a fling and Adam didn't give a rip about Ginger anymore. In fact, he was trying to get rid of her."

"I think he didn't want Ginger for *himself*, but he didn't want anyone *else* to have her, either." Tudy's chin was set with determination.

Lulu said, "What makes you think that Oliver and Ginger were having an affair, Tudy?" Try as she might, she couldn't picture Oliver Hatley and Ginger Cawthorn together.

Tudy's mouth wobbled for a moment until she regained control. "Well, you know how secretive he's been, right? After his fight with Adam that he hasn't even admitted to. He just seemed *sneaky* and that's not like Oliver. The day that Ginger was killed? I'd driven out to Graceland to have lunch with Jeanne after she got off of her docent duty there. And Jeanne and I *saw* them—in a parking lot right on the side of the road."

"Saw them doing *what*?" asked Evelyn with horror.

Tudy waved her hand around. "Saw them *talking*! Does it matter? They were *together*. And I saw her number in his cell phone, too."

Evelyn flushed guiltily. "Oh. I gave Ginger Oliver's cell phone number. She said she had some possible ideas for restaurant openings for him."

Tudy shrugged. "No matter how she got the number, the results would have been the same."

"Tudy, Oliver was in the restaurant just yesterday and Jeanne mentioned that she'd seen him with Ginger—she didn't mention you—and he denied he'd even been there."

"It was him, Lulu. Believe me, I know. I saw them talking together. And I totally lost my appetite after that; I called Jeanne up—she was following me—and told her we'd have to take a rain check on lunch. I went home and took to my bed for the rest of the day. I didn't even lift my head up off the pillow."

Lulu tried to reason with Tudy, who seemed about as stubborn as Lulu had ever seen her. "But what about Ginger? If Oliver killed Adam and was in love with Ginger, then who killed Ginger? It just doesn't make any sense, honey."

Tudy said, "I can tell you haven't been watching *All My Children* lately, Lulu. If you *had* been watching the soaps you'd know that when it comes to love, all your buried passions come bubbling up to the surface. It's clear to me that Oliver killed Ginger. Think about it—she was jolted when Adam was murdered and realized her true feelings for him. She was consumed by guilt and renewed feelings of love! So she told Oliver that they couldn't continue seeing each other. In a fit of rage, Oliver kills Ginger."

Lulu's mouth dropped at this melodramatic logic. "But what about his dental appointment? Oliver says he went to the dentist that afternoon."

Tudy's face darkened. "Except the dentist's office called to tell us they were assessing us with a twenty-five dollar missed appointment fee. So wherever he was, it sure wasn't getting his teeth cleaned."

Evelyn and Lulu both bit their lips to keep from telling Big Jack's story. But a promise was a promise. They both tried to cheer her up by reassuring her that Oliver was devoted to Tudy and would never dream of cheating on her.

Fortunately, a nice distraction unexpectedly came their way or else Lulu would have still desperately been wracking her brain to think up something else to talk about. They were standing in line at the Chinese buffet when Tudy motioned to the back of a man's head.

"Isn't that Holden Parsons? Bless his heart—he's eating at the food court. And him all used to eating at great restaurants all day for his reviews." Tudy pulled a long face. "It makes me sad—it's just like Oliver losing his job. Men without jobs are really like lost souls. They don't know what to do with themselves."

Evelyn was fully in Lady Bountiful mode now. "Let's go over and talk to him. The poor man! Eating fast food when he used to eat out at the best places in town."

Holden, although he was as gracious as usual, looked embarrassed at eating tacos at the food court.

"What are you ladies doing today?" he asked in what Lulu thought was an effort at distracting them from his tacos.

"Evelyn and Tudy were kind enough to help me look

for a dress to wear for a special occasion. Floral-print dresses were apparently not going to cut it," said Lulu.

"Sounds fancy. Where are you going?"

"Oh, Lulu and I are going to Big Jack's fund-raiser at his lake house. Looks to be quite a shindig. The Memphis paper will even be there to write it up," said Evelyn in a careless voice, dipping her egg roll into some soy sauce. She took a bite. "Salty!" and shook her head. But she went right back to dipping the egg roll again.

Holden's eyes widened. "The paper will be there? I've been trying to talk to those guys for a week now—I want to step back into my old job now that Adam isn't writing for them anymore. Think maybe I can somehow get an invitation?"

Lulu said, "Since you're taking up some professional photography assignments, why don't we see if Big Jack would have you come and take pictures at the fund-raiser for your campaign?"

Evelyn slapped the side of the table. "That's perfect! Then you'll have a gig and a chance to butter up the people from the paper and see if you can find out what they're doing about the empty restaurant critic spot."

Tudy frowned. "Won't the paper bring their own photographer?"

Evelyn waved her hand dismissively, "They usually take three or four pictures then head off home. They're not there to provide publicity photos. Big Jack will want good pictures of himself looking mayoral and maybe some with him standing with different local celebrities.

The paper wouldn't be taking those kinds of photos. Here, I'll give him a call."

A few minutes later, she hung up her cell phone, flushed with success. "It's all set. He said it was a brilliant idea! He could use some more pictures for his mailers and his website."

Holden crumpled up his trash and put it on his plastic tray. He beamed at the ladies. "That's wonderful! And I'd never have known if I hadn't seen y'all here today. Thanks, Evelyn! I'll see you and Lulu this weekend."

Evelyn and Lulu said good-bye to Tudy in the parking lot. "Thanks, girls," she said, giving them huge hugs. "You just don't know what good medicine this was for me today. I feel better just having talked to y'all."

As she drove off, Evelyn said, "Lulu? I hate to say this, but you're my private eye, so you need to know. After Tudy saw Oliver with Ginger, she did *not* spend the rest of the day in her bed. I saw her driving around myself—when I was on my way back home from the police department."

Lulu felt her head start pounding. As soon as she wrapped her head around one idea, here came another to set her mind spinning. "Tudy! So . . . you think that *Tudy* might have killed Ginger? Because she was jealous or worried that she was going to take Oliver away from her?" Lulu was quiet for a moment. "Evelyn, I somehow just can't picture Tudy pulling out a gun and blowing someone away."

"She could do it, Lulu. Remember—Tudy grew up in Texas."

Lulu frowned at her in puzzlement.

"*Don't mess with Texas*—those women know how to shoot . . . and straight, too. Tudy wouldn't spare a second thought for Ginger if she'd been messing with her marriage."

Lulu was glad to have Big Jack's fund-raiser as a distraction from the case. Her head was still swimming from all the suspect possibilities and she still hated to think that one of her friends was responsible for two murders.

Lulu was also glad she'd gone shopping when she saw all the gussied-up people at Big Jack's fund-raiser. Lulu had a feeling that most of the dresses there cost more than her mortgage payment.

The party was in Big Jack's expansive backyard, smack-dab on the lake. The caterers had put up huge tents strung with strings of white lights. The band was a short ways away (so it was easier for people to talk) playing a set of crowd favorites, judging from the dancing on the floor set up under a separate tent.

Big Jack looked to be in hog heaven. He was laughing his big, hearty laugh, shaking hands right and left, and politicking just as hard as he could. If there *had* been babies there, he'd have kissed every single one of them. He was in his element.

Lulu felt like she was in her element, too. Not being around the chichi people or the glamorous designer clothing—but the food. There were crab cakes, cremini mushrooms, roasted carrots, and pan-roasted duck. But Lulu's favorite were the jumbo shrimp glazed with a homemade peach sauce that melted in her mouth. "Evelyn," said Lulu with a happy sigh, "I've died and gone to epicurean heaven. Have you tried these shrimp?"

Evelyn said, "No, I fixed myself a vegetable plate. I'm not ordinarily a girl who loads up with a lot of greens, but these creamy collards are the best things I think I've ever put in my mouth. Aunt Pat's barbeque aside, of course."

Lulu nodded, "Oh, Aunt Pat's recipes are marvelous— but this food is *special*." She walked to a buffet area lined with chafing dishes to see what other wonders were being offered. She bet she could figure out that peach sauce for the shrimp. It wouldn't work well for the barbeque restaurant, but she sure would love to serve it for a party.

A few hours later, guests finally started leaving. Lulu and Evelyn had already taken off their heels and were chatting and people watching. Lulu was about as stuffed as she'd ever been.

Holden walked up to them, beaming.

"How did the photography go tonight, Holden?" asked Lulu.

"It looked like it was going *great* to me," said Evelyn, after taking a swallow from her wineglass. "Every time I saw Holden, he was taking a picture of Big Jack with some bigwig or other. And Big Jack's grins made him look like the cat that ate the canary."

Big Jack sauntered up in time to catch the end of

what Evelyn said. "Amen to that. I *did* eat some canaries. This has been my most successful fund-raiser ever. And Holden, great job recording the moments. I should have some fantastic pictures for my campaign flyers."

Holden smiled modestly. "It *did* seem to go well, I have to admit. Everybody acted like they wanted to pose."

Evelyn laughed. "Well, of course they do! They're all gussied up and look like a million dollars. After all the money they spent on manicures, pedicures, and dresses and hair, they *want* it memorialized for all time!"

"It surely went much better than my last gig. Oh, sorry, Lulu." Holden's bald head turned pink.

"Taking the pictures for Aunt Pat's didn't go well?" asked Lulu, surprised. "I didn't think that would be a problem."

"It wasn't! At least, taking pictures of the restaurant and downtown Memphis wasn't a problem. But then I took some snapshots of *people*—you know, like we talked about. For the wedding party to see before they hired me? Some people just flat-out told me that they didn't want their picture taken. Maybe if folks aren't looking their best, they're not as wild about having their picture taken."

Holden fidgeted a moment, then said, "And taking pictures can make more trouble than just complaints from unwilling subjects. Before we even talked about my taking pictures professionally, Lulu, I followed Ginger around for a couple of days to try to take some pictures of her." He gulped. "She'd just irritated the stew out of me the day before and I thought I'd tail her and see if I could irritate her back by maybe catching her in some sort of compromising moment or doing something bad. Maybe even something illegal."

Lulu took a deep breath. "When you were taking these pictures . . . were they right before her murder?"

"Not *right* before, but I did snap some from that day. But then I went off to lunch after that, so I didn't see anything that would help the police out." Holden looked like he couldn't decide whether that was a good thing or not. "I mean, the last thing I took was her talking to Oliver in that parking lot."

Lulu said sharply, "You actually *saw* the two of them together?"

"Saw them? Yes—I even took a picture of them. I thought it was kind of weird to see them together. I didn't think they weren't friends or anything. And it didn't exactly look much like a friendly discussion. They were waving their hands around, their faces were red, and Ginger looked like she was yelling."

Big Jack interrupted loudly, "You know, Holden, I bet you totally misinterpreted what you saw. They were probably just shopping at the same place and started talking in the parking lot. And maybe it looked like they weren't getting along because they were talking about Adam—Oliver wasn't Adam's biggest fan and maybe Ginger was singing his praises like she'd been doing at the funeral. But it doesn't mean that Oliver was about to shoot Ginger."

Holden said quickly, "No, of course it doesn't. Like I

said, it wasn't even at the time of the murder—and it was on the other side of town. I just thought it was odd seeing them together, that's all."

"Shouldn't you turn the pictures over to the police?" asked Lulu hesitantly. "They'd want anything that might help them piece together Ginger's last day."

Big Jack said with a big laugh, "Which sounds like a good thing to do, Holden, until you think about what you just said. You were irritated with Ginger so you followed her around with a camera to take pictures and irritate her back. And you were with her the day she died. Might want to rethink turning them in, you know?"

Holden cringed. "No. No, Lulu, I don't want anything to do with that. It's not going to help the police out anyway—there's nothing there."

"Do you mind if *I* see the pictures, though? I'd like to just take a closer look, that's all. Maybe there's something in the pictures that can give us a clue," said Lulu.

Evelyn cracked up. "You should see your face, Holden! Didn't you know that Lulu was trading in her spatula for a magnifying glass? She's a crime investigator now . . . mostly to help me out." Evelyn, deep in her wineglass now, gave Lulu a tight hug. "She's the best friend *ever*. And if I manage to keep out of jail, I'll owe it all to her."

Holden nodded. "I see. Well, I've got them on the camera and I could e-mail them to you when I get back home, so you could see them. I was planning on taking a closer look at them myself, anyway. Then I'll send them over to you."

Big Jack said, "I've got a great idea, y'all. Now that the guests have left, why don't we head out on the boat for a while? It's the perfect night for a boat ride. We could bring a little food with us—and some wine bottles of course."

"I'd love to go, but I can't swim," said Holden. "Which isn't ideal for a boat ride." He gave a nervous laugh.

"I have life vests," Big Jack offered.

"Maybe next time? I probably need to be getting back, anyway—it's a long drive home and I'm not staying at the lake like y'all are."

After he left, Evelyn said, "I guess I should feel bad about not offering to let him stay at my place. But it wouldn't have been as much fun as a girls' weekend. Plus I have a feeling that we'd be listening to his hard-luck story about getting kicked out of his newspaper job the whole time."

The night was warm, but the boat cutting through the water on the lake stirred up a breeze that made Lulu fold her arms up to her chest.

Evelyn, used to boat excursions on her own ski boat, curled up into a corner and was asleep in less than five minutes.

Lisa, Big Jack's wife, stayed behind to talk to the caterers but packed up a plate of food before the boat

pulled away. Although Lulu had thought she'd never
eat again after all the delicious food she'd put away, she
somehow couldn't resist munching on moist cheese biscuits. As the boat moved through the water, she looked
at the huge houses lining the lake. All of them were lit
up like they were having parties, too. And the moon sat
right above the horizon, casting a glow on the water that
looked like a path leading right up to it.

Big Jack cleared his throat and said, "Evelyn?" When
there was no response from the napping Evelyn, he cut
the engine and threw out an anchor. The boat gently
rocked and Evelyn let out a small snore.

"I wanted to talk to you about something, Lulu, but I
didn't want to do it in front of Evelyn." Big Jack sat next
to Lulu at the front of the boat and spoke to her in a low
voice. "You see, I've been real worried about a couple of
things and I haven't known what to do about it."

Lulu dabbed her mouth with a napkin. "What kinds
of things? You mean, with the murders?"

Big Jack nodded, pushing a strand of thick, black hair
off his forehead. "I've solved those murders, Lulu. I've
been thinking about it a lot because I was worried about
both Oliver and Evelyn being accused. And Oliver had
absolutely nothing to do with it. You know that, right?"
He looked right in Lulu's eyes. "I know I told you about
how crazy he'd been acting right after Adam died, but
he was just so shocked that he'd pushed Adam down the
stairs. But he's totally free and clear."

He seemed to be waiting for Lulu to acknowledge
that fact, so Lulu nodded. But inside she wasn't so sure.

Maybe Big Jack wasn't so sure, either, but he was trying to keep his cousin from being a major suspect in a murder case—which couldn't possibly be good for a mayoral campaign. Especially since Oliver had gotten Big Jack involved by showing up on his doorstep.

"And then I was worried that *I* was suspected of murdering Adam. Just because of that answering-machine message. Thank God the police haven't let anything leak out to the press; the newspapers would have a field day if they thought I was caught up in blackmail and murder." Big Jack scowled at the idea.

"What do you think happened?" asked Lulu, tilting her head to one side and endangering the bun of white hair that was carefully wound up on the top of her head.

"I think Ginger killed Adam. Don't *you*? She was one mad filly at that guy, and she had every right to be. He'd done her wrong—out in public and everything. I mean, he also cheated on Evelyn, but they weren't *married*. Well, not married at that moment, anyway—I know Evelyn *used* to be married to him. Ginger was breathing fire, though, that he'd broken up their marriage and was seeing another woman . . . or two."

Lulu looked off toward the shore and Big Jack sighed.

"I know what you're thinking," he said. "You think that's real hypocritical of me, considering Adam was blackmailing me for the same thing. But from everything I've heard, Adam was real ugly to Ginger. That's not the way I treat ladies."

What a gentleman, thought Lulu wryly. She wasn't so

sure that Big Jack's wife, Lisa, would feel the same way about his cheating. But she smiled at him.

"So you think Ginger got fed up with Adam's attitude and shot him?"

Big Jack pointed a thick finger at her. "That's *exactly* what I think happened. I think maybe she was having an argument with him, he mouthed off at her, and she had a gun with her and took him out. I don't think it was something she planned on doing, but it was something she was *prepared* to do."

"She sure seemed all cut up about it, though. She said she wanted to memorialize him forever, and avenge his death and all of that."

Big Jack shrugged. "Self-protection. If she acts like someone else needs to be caught, then she's diverted suspicion from herself. And I think the lady knew how to put on an act."

"But that still doesn't explain Ginger's death. If Ginger killed Adam, then who killed Ginger? And why?"

Big Jack looked bored. He shrugged his big shoulders. "She was probably a victim of a random act of violence. You know? Maybe some punk was planning on robbing her; she got her back up and wasn't going to let him take her purse. And then he shot her—but got too freaked out to take her wallet."

It was one explanation, but it just didn't seem right to Lulu.

"There was something else I wanted to tell you," said Big Jack, looking surreptitiously at the sleeping Evelyn at the other end of the boat. "I've been worried about our mutual friend over there."

Lulu's heart skipped a beat. "What do you mean?"

Big Jack opened his mouth, and then snapped it shut again and shook his head.

"Now you *know* you have to tell me now! What's wrong with Evelyn?"

Big Jack looked broodingly at the water. "She's a great friend of mine, Lulu. She's helped build up my political career over the years. Even when I was just scraping by and stumping in the street, she always slipped me a little cash to help me out. She gave me more than just financial support, too—she talked me up to her fancy friends and introduced me to the right people. She's been a huge help to me."

Lulu tried not to be impatient. "So, spit it out, Big Jack. What's wrong?"

He sighed again. "Okay. Well, I gave you my favorite scenario of what happened to Adam and Ginger. And that's really what I'm telling myself I believe. But I did see Evelyn the day that Ginger died. And she was having a big argument with her."

Lulu relaxed a little. "Oh. Don't you worry about *that*, Big Jack. The police know all about Evelyn and Ginger's argument outside that Beale Street restaurant. Pink was talking to Evelyn about it that same day. Some witnesses described a woman that looked just like Evelyn. And she did own up to it—but says that Ginger was very much alive when she left her."

Big Jack hesitated again. "But see . . . that's not where
I saw them argue. My law office is right down the street,
right? I saw her outside the parking garage. And she was
waving around this pretty, tiny little gun. Looked like
a toy."

Lulu swallowed hard. "But Ginger was shot *inside*
the parking garage. Not outside. And why the hell didn't
you phone the police, Big Jack? You could've stopped
her before anything even happened."

He lifted up his big, pawlike hands. "Now hold on
a minute, Lulu. *I* didn't do anything wrong here. I'm
just telling you what I saw. Anyway, I saw her put the
gun back in her purse. So I thought that maybe I just
misinterpreted what I saw. Maybe they were just having
this really animated discussion and Evelyn was showing
Ginger her new gun."

He shrugged helplessly. "I don't know. Maybe they
were acting out a possible scenario for when Adam was
murdered, since Ginger was trying to avenge his death.
Believe me, I don't want Evelyn to end up being the
murderer—and I had no intention of calling the police
when I saw her with a gun. The woman practically made
me and my political career. She's one of my biggest donors. Of *course* I didn't want to call the cops."

Lulu looked over at the sleeping Evelyn. "I just don't
believe she had anything to do with it."

"I don't, either. I *don't*," he said quickly, in a firm
voice. "But I felt like I needed to tell somebody about it.
And there's more."

Lulu's heart sank.

"She hasn't been acting like herself since these murders, Lulu. Admit it, you've noticed it, too! She's smoking like a house afire—have you ever seen her smoke before?"

Lulu hadn't.

"Her drinking has gotten a lot heavier, too. This makes me think there's something giving her a whole lot of stress and she's dealing with it by developing some bad habits."

Lulu said eagerly, "But it *has* been stressful—the whole thing, Big Jack! She was in love with Adam. She even thought they might get married again. She was absolutely crushed when she saw him cheating on her. And furious that he was cheating on her with her own money funding his dates. Then Adam died and Evelyn had to deal with guilt feelings about being furious with him and having him die. Then she became a suspect in Adam's murder—if that's not stressful, I don't know what is."

Big Jack didn't look convinced. Lulu continued, "She became friends with Ginger, but that whole friendship was stressful, too. Ginger had a different opinion of Adam from Evelyn—she wanted to avenge Adam's death and Evelyn was looking to heal from their horrible breakup."

Big Jack said, "But Ginger really *didn't* want to avenge Adam's death."

"But Evelyn didn't know that. So the whole situation was very strange for her. And then Ginger dies a violent death on top of everything else going on. So then she'd lost a friend, too."

Big Jack rubbed his forehead slowly. "I'd like to believe those are the only reasons she's acting so different.

Between her smoking and drinking, she's definitely upset about something. I hope you're right that it's just regular stress and not that she's murdered Adam or Ginger—or both of them. I don't need to lose my biggest donor—and she's a personal friend, too."

Lulu said quietly, "I hope I'm right, too."

Chapter

15

Tommie was up early the next morning, banging around in the kitchen and efficiently pulling together a hearty breakfast.

Lulu, used to many years of early rising for Aunt Pat's, got right up. Evelyn had cleverly designed the house so her bedroom was farthest from the noises of the kitchen, thus enabling her favorite activity—sleeping in.

Like Evelyn's Memphis kitchen, the lake-house edition was the kind of kitchen you could get lost in. It was completely covered with the finest granite and hand-crafted wooden cabinets. But what really amazed Lulu were both the huge amount of kitchen equipment—from serious knife sets to steamers and processors—and the fact that everything had a place inside a cabinet. Lulu had some great kitchen tools at her small kitchen at home, but half of them lived on her countertop.

Tommie smiled at her, nodding her head at Lulu as she whisked eggs over a large china bowl. "I kind of thought you might be the first one up, Miss Lulu. Miss Evelyn isn't one for getting up early unless she's not feeling well and needs a coffee and a water for her headache."

Lulu laughed. "I gathered that about her. But you know, she might be feeling a little bit under the weather this morning, so I wouldn't be too surprised to see her in the kitchen."

Tommie stopped whisking. "Don't tell me. Too much drinking? Was she in bad shape?"

Lulu shook her head. "Not *so* bad. But enough to make her sleepy. She fell asleep on Big Jack's boat last night. I drove the car back to the house, actually. But after all the food we ate last night, I think everybody was sleepy."

Tommie set her lips together in a thin line and whacked the whisk against the side of the bowl.

Lulu decided it might be a good idea to change the subject. "The food last night was delicious, Tommie. I live most of my life at a restaurant, but this was totally different. The presentation on the plates was gorgeous. And the food absolutely melted in your mouth. The peach sauce was to die for. And they had haricots verts." Lulu looked innocently at Tommie, knowing she was going to pooh-pooh the last food.

She wasn't disappointed. Tommie snorted. "Haricots verts, my big toe! We're here in America and here in America they're *green beans*. Or string beans. Or snap beans. Fancying them all up to be haricots."

"Well, whatever they were, they sure were good. They were a little bit thinner than the snap beans I grow in my garden. And they didn't look anything at all like the way I usually fix them. . . . You know, I let them sit in a soup pot all day with a ham hock and put some brown sugar in there with them to stew for a while."

Tommie nodded. "Of course you do. That's how snap beans are supposed to be fixed."

"Well, they fixed them a little different. They'd cut up some summer tomatoes in there and some green onion. I thought I tasted some lemon, too. I'm going to have to fix them that way myself, the next time I cook them." Tommie looked unconvinced. "It's all New South cooking, Tommie."

Tommie sniffed. "Well, I'm sure I don't know what was wrong with Old South cooking. Don't you go and get too elegant for us, Miss Lulu. We need as many down-home cooks as we can get right now. And country food satisfies me a lot longer than some of that classy cooking. The main thing I have a problem with at those fancy restaurants is the way they think that if it's pretty enough, it doesn't even matter how much they put on the plate. Like it's art or something. It's *nice* if it's pretty. I understand where they're coming from with that. But it doesn't mean I want just a tiny dab of it. I don't like seeing any white spaces on my plates. If I'm serving somebody a special meal, I want them to have enough food to be able to *taste* it. And they can have as much as they like, too. If they want seconds? Well, then, that's just a compliment to the cook as far as I'm concerned."

Lulu hid a smile. Tommie definitely subscribed to the "more is better" philosophy of food. Lulu didn't think she'd ever gotten a plate from Tommie's capable hands that wasn't positively groaning with delicious food. "What treat are you delighting my taste buds with this morning, Tommie?"

"Honey, I've got you something that's going to start your day off with a bang. This here is my special grits breakfast casserole. A big helping of this and you are going to be set for food for your day."

Lulu's tummy rumbled on cue. "So I'm guessing some eggs, grits, shredded cheese, and maybe some sausage?"

"And not just that—but a box of cornbread mix. That's going to give it some sweetness, you know. 'Cause we need something sweet at the start of the day to help us get going."

Lulu sighed in anticipation as she poured herself a cup of coffee from the impressive-looking coffeemaker on the granite countertop. "What about Evelyn? Do you think the sausage will sit well with her? She might be feeling a little puny this morning."

Tommie looked grim again. "Well, I'm used to this nonsense, so I have both hot and mild sausage in the fridge. I'll be nice this time and pull out the mild one. Although maybe she deserves a taste of the spicy stuff."

Lulu put some cream in her coffee and a spoonful of sugar. She sat at the kitchen table, stirring the coffee. "I did want to ask you about Evelyn a little, Tommie. Do you think she's doing okay?"

Tommie snorted. "She sure seems okay to me! Going

out and partying and all kinds of foolishness. I'm not feeling too sorry for her, that's for sure."

"But do you think it's normal for her to be acting this way?" pressed Lulu.

Tommie, frying up the sausage, looked over her shoulder at Lulu. "She's always been someone who enjoys her cocktails, Miss Lulu. Do *you* think there's something wrong?"

"Not really," said Lulu slowly. "It's just that she's started up smoking again and then last night she did act like she'd had a lot to drink." Lulu shook her head and then took a big sip from her coffee. "Just ignore me, Tommie. Everybody lets off steam now and again. And Evelyn's had a lot of steam to let off."

"That Adam was the devil himself," said Tommie darkly. "He's the reason she's been so upset lately. Then that Ginger, who was just about as bad. I don't know where a lady like Miss Evelyn picks these thugs up."

Lulu hesitated. "You haven't ever seen Evelyn with a gun, have you, Tommie?"

Tommie looked sharply at Lulu as she drained the grease from the sausage. "No, ma'am, I haven't! What makes you think that Miss Evelyn is toting a weapon around?"

"Big Jack last night. I was talking to him on the boat . . . while Evelyn was sleeping. He said he'd seen her having an argument with Ginger the day she was killed. He said that Evelyn looked furious and was waving a gun around."

"Bah! I don't believe a word of it. If *anybody* had a

gun, it would be that Ginger. She was probably around
nasty people all day and needed a gun to protect herself
from their filthiness."

"But wouldn't Ginger have a serious-looking gun?
It does sound a little more like Evelyn to be carrying
something around that's dainty looking."

Evelyn was pouring the hot grits, cooked sausage,
and eggs into a big casserole dish and mixing it together
with the box of cornbread. It seemed to be an activity
that was taking all of her concentration. Or maybe she
was just figuring out what she was going to say.

"You could tell me that you saw Miss Evelyn shoot
Ginger in the back with your very own eyes and I
wouldn't believe a word that came out of your mouth.
I'd be convinced you'd had a strong cocktail at lunch
or that your new medication was interactin' poorly with
your daily vitamin. I'd know you were *wrong*. And this
is just wrong, Miss Lulu. Besides, there's not an inch of
this house or the main house that I don't know in and
out and top to bottom. There's not a handgun anywhere
in either one."

Lulu opened her mouth to tell Tommie what Big Jack
had said but shut it again as Tommie suddenly cocked
her head to one side like she was listening and held up
a hand. She smoothly slid the casserole into the oven as
Evelyn sleepily entered the kitchen in a silk bathrobe.

She covered a yawn, then said, "Sausage? Something
smells good."

"Grits breakfast casserole," said Tommie. "It'll be
ready in about thirty minutes, honey."

Evelyn was already pouring herself a large cup of coffee. "Tommie, do you know where the aspirin is?" She made a face at Lulu. "Sad, isn't it? That wine from last night is talking back to me." She took a big swallow of coffee and rolled her head around to loosen her neck. "Have y'all been telling secrets this morning?"

Lulu guiltily looked away. But Tommie took out her dish towel and started cleaning up the countertop. "Don't be silly. What secrets would a respectable lady like Miss Lulu possibly have?"

Evelyn snorted. "I don't know, Tommie. But how well do we *really* know someone? Maybe Lulu has her own secret life. We just *think* she's a mild-mannered owner of a favorite local barbeque establishment. But in *reality*, she's an international spy, using Aunt Pat's as a home base. Or," she added grimly, "maybe she's a restaurant critic. It would be a perfect cover. Who'd ever guess that a reviewer would be a restaurant owner, too?"

Lulu and Tommie exchanged glances. "What a thing to say, Miss Evelyn! You've just got restaurant critics on the brain, that's all."

Evelyn glumly stared down at the kitchen table. "I guess. Although that's perfectly understandable, isn't it? And, really, I think I'm more into secret lives instead of restaurant reviewers. Because that was the first shock—finding out that Adam was a restaurant critic instead of just a former restaurant owner. Like Holden."

Lulu said soothingly, "But everybody knew that Holden was a restaurant critic. I remember seeing him come into Aunt Pat's. He had his little notebook and pencil with him and proceeded to look around the dining room, making notes. Nothing obvious about that, right?" Lulu hooted.

Evelyn said, "Maybe we all knew what Holden was back then, but I'm not so sure what he is now. He was always just this innocuous bald little man with an old-fashioned suit and a bow tie. Meek and mild. Now all he thinks about is getting back with the newspaper. He was trying to talk to get his old job back at Adam's funeral, and then he was talking to some of those men from the paper last night at Big Jack's fund-raiser."

Lulu frowned. "I thought he was acting really professional last night. Every time I looked over at him, he was taking a picture of Big Jack with his arm around somebody important."

Evelyn said, "Yes, but he *also* found time to ask the newspaper men to put in a good word for him at the paper. He was working all the angles."

"Networking," said Tommie decidedly. "That's what that is. No secrets there. Just a man who lost his job who needs to work. That's all there is to it. Why're you trying to make some big deal out of it, honey?"

"There's something fishy about him," persisted Evelyn. "Remember how he got upset with Ginger and decided to follow her around with a camera while he was building up his portfolio? And so he took a bunch of pictures of her . . . but stopped taking them just a couple of hours before her violent death? I just don't see it."

"So what do you think happened," asked Lulu.

"I think he was so mad when Ben told him about

Adam being the new restaurant critic that he packed heat, tracked him down, and shot him. Ginger had aggravated him about something, too. . . . Maybe she caught him taking pictures of her and antagonized him again. So then the hothead in him got all riled up and he shot her."

Lulu wasn't about to argue with Evelyn when she was all wound up like she was. Plus the fact that Evelyn hadn't had her full morning requirement of coffee yet and was hung over from the night before.

"Well," Lulu said slowly. "It *could* have happened that way. Who knows, maybe it did."

"That's my story and I'm sticking with it!" said Evelyn decidedly.

"I meant to ask you, Evelyn," said Lulu, "about something I heard that you and Ginger talked about. Something about Ginger knowing that someone came to a meeting with Adam prepared to kill him?"

"Now who on earth could possibly know about that conversation?" asked Evelyn, folding her arms across her chest. "I swear, sometimes I think Aunt Pat's has ears. Anyway, yes, she did say something like that to me. I didn't mention it to you because it sounded like such a 'duh' moment for Ginger. The man was shot to death—*yes*, someone *did* meet with him prepared to kill him."

"I guess she meant that she *knew* who had come prepared to kill him. Do you think she meant Oliver?" Lulu thoughtfully pursed her lips, and then continued. "We know he was upset with Adam and that he was mad enough to push him down the stairs. Was he *also* mad enough to carry a gun?"

Evelyn made a shooing motion. "I still say it's Holden. After all, he was furious with Adam. He had gobs of motive."

Evelyn was clearly done with all discussion on the murder because she moved with great determination onto other topics of conversation, saying, "Tommie, I'm going to take a peek at those grits. I'm thinking they've got to be done. They *smell* done."

Tommie reared up. "Don't you be messing around in my oven! Get!" She waved a spatula around threateningly as the buzzer went off.

"See!" said Evelyn. "It was done, after all."

Considering all the delicious food she'd enjoyed the night before, Lulu was shocked at how much breakfast casserole she was able to put away. But it was scrumptious. The cornbread mix added that sweetness that Tommie had mentioned, and the grits and eggs made it filling. Lulu gave a happy sigh. This was one recipe she was going to make sure to take back home with her.

No matter how much fun Lulu had when she left town, she always breathed a sigh of relief when she came home again. After a relaxing morning in Evelyn's hammock, Tommie made a delicious arugula and peach salad with a chive vinaigrette for lunch before they headed back to Memphis. Evelyn dropped her off at home, and as Lulu happily walked inside her front door, across the old, creaky hardwoods, and smelled the mixture of old wood and old books that permeated the air, she smiled to herself. Home sweet home.

The drive home had made her a little sleepier than usual. When she looked at the clock and saw it was only seven thirty, she decided to try to stay up a little longer and read for a while.

Lulu would have sworn that she hadn't fallen asleep. The last thing she remembered before the phone rang was being curled up on her plaid sofa with her head propped up with the overstuffed pillows. She'd covered her legs with one of Aunt Pat's old knitted afghans, put on her reading glasses, and opened up her book.

When the phone buzzed abruptly into the hush of Lulu's house, she jolted awake. Blinking, she looked around for it. It felt like the middle of the night, but when Lulu glanced at the clock, it was still a little before midnight. She'd been asleep for hours! Her skin prickled with unease; nobody ever called her past nine o'clock when she was at home.

"Hello?" she asked sharply. She didn't recognize the number on the caller ID.

"Hi," said an odd, disguised-sounding voice. "This is a friend."

Lulu's heart started throbbing hard in her chest. "What friend? Who is this?"

"Never mind who," said the strange voice. "Just listen. Stop nosing around in the murders or you'll be next."

"Who *is* . . ." started Lulu, but there was a click, indicating that the caller had hung up.

Lulu was shaking. She didn't have a clue who'd been on the phone, but she knew one thing—she didn't want to be alone. The shadows of her home suddenly all seemed sinister. With trembling fingers, she dialed Ben and Sara.

Sara picked up the phone and sounded like she'd been awake. "Lulu? What's going on?"

The story spilled out of Lulu while Sara listened intently on the other end until Sara broke in. "I'm coming over, Lulu! Just hold on tight."

◇◇◇◇◇◇◇◇◇◇◇◇◇◇◇◇◇◇◇

In the end, Ben came over, too, after telling Derrick to keep an ear out for the twins. Ben looked rumpled and half awake but concerned.

"I'm sorry," said Lulu as they hurried through her kitchen door. "This is the one night that we're not all working at the restaurant late and I'm calling and walking y'all up!"

Sara gave her a hug. "I was still awake actually. Reading a scary book—until you called me with something even scarier."

Ben said, sitting down at Lulu's kitchen table, "What I don't understand, Mother, is why this person called. You haven't been nosing into anything, have you?" He put both hands palms up, beseechingly. "I mean, *tell* me you haven't been getting mixed up in all this."

Lulu said, "No more mixed up than I was last time, Ben."

"But last time, Mother, you were mixed all the way up to your neck in it!"

Lulu sighed. "I've just been supportive, that's all, Ben. I'm trying to look out for you and Evelyn. I figured if I could find out who did it, then you and Evelyn will be cleared and we can all go back to worrying about barbeque."

Ben said, "I can tell you right now that the police are *not* going to pull me in for killing Adam Cawthorn. Yes, he gave us a lousy review. Yes, it made me mad that he put down my cooking, because that's the one thing in life that I know I'm really good at. But the reason they're not going to connect me with his murder or with

Ginger's is because I have absolutely nothing to do with it. And they won't be able to find a scrap of evidence otherwise. Just because Daddy was a scoundrel doesn't mean I'm one, too, Mother."

Sara rubbed her freckled forehead like it hurt. "Remind me again why someone wants to kill you, Lulu?"

Lulu sighed. "It's probably due to the fact that Evelyn has been telling everybody who'll listen that I'm such a great friend and that I'm her secret weapon against the police."

"Secret . . ." Sara frowned.

"Yes. She asked me to act like her private investigator. I guess she thought it up because I solved the case last time and she's my friend."

Ben said, "Who exactly has heard her mention that you're investigating the murder for her?"

Lulu gave a short laugh. "Oh, probably everybody! And whoever *hasn't* heard her say it has heard Peggy Sue say it—she's like the gossip Greek chorus, you know. Always echoing anything you say. I love her, but that's just the way she is. Chatty."

Sara pushed her riotous red curls out of her face to look closer at Lulu. "So what *do* you know? Maybe we can figure out who is trying to scare you off."

"That's the thing—I really *don't* know all that much. Holden threw baked beans at Adam and took pictures of Ginger, but swears he didn't do anything. Oliver pushed Adam down the stairs and had a heated argument with Ginger. Evelyn trashed Adam's apartment, discovered his body, and argued with Ginger the day she died. Big Jack was determined not to pay Adam blackmail money anymore and his office isn't far from where Adam's body was found. Ginger could have continued blackmailing Big Jack, but he was out of town the afternoon she was murdered. Tudy was convinced that Oliver was having an affair with Ginger—and she wasn't where she was supposed to be." Lulu threw up her hands. "I really don't know anything!"

But as she said the words, something struck her as a little bit off. She felt like there was something she should be paying closer attention to there. Lulu frowned.

Sara yawned loudly. "Lulu, I'm with you—I don't know a thing, either. Ben, why don't you just run back home. I'll stay here overnight with Lulu. And I'm so tired and cross that I just dare a murderer to try to mess with me right now."

"Psst!"

Lulu frowned and looked around. Then she smiled and looked *lower*. Because only nine-year-old Ella Beth would actually make a sound like that.

Sure enough, Ella Beth was underneath a table. Lulu, who couldn't quite get down that low, sat down at the booth. "What's up, sugar?" she asked in a low voice. "Got some information for me?"

"Yes, Granny Lulu, I do. But can we arrange to meet somewhere else? 'Cause right now it looks like you're talking to yourself and I don't want you to attract any attention. People will think you've gone crazy. I'll meet you back in the office."

"Oh, okay." Lulu looked around a little self-consciously. No one seemed to be looking her way, though.

Ella Beth looked carefully around the office, even under the desk. "You never know when someone might be listening in," she said.

Like Ella Beth, thought Lulu.

"So what have you got for me, Agent Ella Beth?"

"I've heard all kinds of things, Granny Lulu. As my sidekick, I'm going to share a little bit of what I've learned. And this is from many hours of hiding under tables, behind chairs, and around corners."

"Okay, shoot," said Lulu, settling into the office's comfy old sofa.

"Well, Cherry dyes her hair. She goes to the beauty parlor twice a month to get it that color. So . . . she's kind of in disguise."

Lulu hid a smile. Cherry had hair the same shade of henna as Lucy Ricardo. No one but a child would think it was natural.

Lulu pulled a thoughtful face, stroking her chin. "So you think Cherry might have done it."

Ella Beth said reluctantly, "Well, no, not really. Because Cherry is just great and I can't see her doing something like that. Or, even if she *did* do it, I think she'd march right over to the police station and tell them. She wouldn't let little kids find a body like that."

"True," agreed Lulu.

"And then I also found out what Coco is getting for her birthday! And Mama and Daddy never tell me because they think I can't keep a secret. And they're *wrong*. But that doesn't really have anything to do with the mystery. I just thought it was interesting."

"Which it *is*," said Lulu. "Maybe you can tell your folks right before Coco opens her presents that you knew exactly what she's getting and have kept quiet about it the whole time."

"Great idea! I knew you'd make a good sidekick," said Ella Beth, freckled face beaming. "And let's see what else. I heard Peggy Sue complaining about how many bills she had and did the electric company think she was made of money? Should she have to pay an arm and a leg just to keep herself cool?"

"Which is a good question." Lulu nodded. "It's so hot in Memphis that it takes a lot of electricity to keep us comfy, I guess."

"And then I heard Mr. Parsons talking to Cherry about that woman . . . Miz Cawthorn? The one he'd been arguing with the last time. This was right before you went to the lake."

Lulu leaned forward a little. "Is that so?"

"Well, it started off that Cherry—see, she *might* be a bad guy—started complaining about Miz Cawthorn. She said 'I don't like to talk ill of the dead, but I think she got what was coming to her.' Or something like that." She looked reproachfully at Lulu. "You didn't tell me she was dead. How can I solve the case if my own sidekick isn't sharing things with me?"

"I'm sorry," said Lulu, chastened. "I didn't want to make you upset, sugar."

"But I didn't find *her* body," said Ella Beth, calmly looking at Lulu. "I'm only upset if I know the person or if I find a body. Anyway, so Cherry said, 'Ginger's whole personality just stank.'

"And then Mr. Parsons, who was eating his peach cobbler the whole time, and Cherry were talking about the pictures he'd taken the day Miz Cawthorn died. And how he thought maybe he could find some clues to the murder in the pictures." Ella Beth looked at Lulu sadly. "Everyone thinks they can be a detective. But there was something else that was interesting, Granny Lulu. I wasn't the only one listening in on Mr. Parsons and Cherry."

"You weren't, honey?"

"Guess who else was listening to them."

"Coco?"

"No!" said Ella Beth. "It was Big Jack. He was sitting in the next booth, right behind them. He was sitting really still and listening to every single word."

Lulu chewed over her conversation with Ella Beth while she packed up to-go boxes in the kitchen. She bet Big Jack had really perked up when he heard Oliver's name. She'd noticed how protective he was of his cousin when they were talking about him at the lake. She remembered his easy assurances that Holden had misinterpreted what he'd seen. Since Big Jack had eavesdropped, he'd had a heads-up that Holden had seen Oliver and what he thought about it.

Lulu wondered what Oliver would do when he found out. Could he have possibly killed Ginger? And why? Was he really having the affair with Ginger that Tudy was so certain about? Or maybe . . . Pink had said that Ginger and Adam were in on the blackmailing gig together. Did Ginger have something to blackmail Oliver over? But Oliver hadn't had any contact with Adam until he found out Adam was the critic who he blamed for his restaurant's failure. Had Oliver killed Adam—and Ginger knew about it? But then what would he do when he found out about Holden?

Could Oliver have returned to the parking garage to make sure that Adam was as dead as he'd looked? Then, when he saw the body was gone, could he have tried again—and been successful? Ella Beth's mention of the pictures reminded Lulu to ask Holden to e-mail her the photographs so she could take a closer look at them.

Her thoughts were interrupted when Derrick came slouching past Lulu, headphones firmly entrenched in his ears. Lulu reached out and held his arm. He unplugged himself and gave Lulu a small smile, and she said, "Sugar, I just wanted to ask you how everything went the other night with Peaches. Did y'all have a good time at the movie? It looked like things were going okay over dinner." Well, thought Lulu, besides Jeanne swearing up and down to Oliver that she'd seen him with the murdered Ginger.

Derrick shrugged and looked around the dining room uncomfortably.

"Let's talk in the office," said Lulu. "I think the girls are playing with the Labs on the porch."

The office was quiet enough for Derrick to open up a little more. "It was okay, I guess. She was real nice and . . . well, she was pretty."

"She sure was," said Lulu, nodding.

"The only thing was that I didn't really know what to say, you know? I felt like I was real boring."

Lulu squinted at him. "She didn't look bored when I saw her, Derrick. She looked like she was having a real nice conversation with you."

"Yeah, but she had to start the conversation every single time! I was like a bump on a log. I don't know—I just felt panicked or something."

"But teenage girls are used to that, honey. Believe me! Teenage boys aren't known for being great conversationalists. The girls always have to carry the weight of the conversation."

"I guess." Derrick's scowl looked far from certain.

"She's interested in *you*, Derrick. You know how women love those strong, silent types. She wants to find out more about what *you're* all about."

Derrick gave a short laugh. "Good luck to her, then. Because I don't really know what I'm all about, either."

Lulu wanted to give him a big hug, but she had a feeling that a hug wasn't what Derrick was in the mood for right now. "Honey, we all felt that way as teenagers. Maybe she's interested in finding out more about you *with* you. You have so much promise and potential—don't ignore all the things you've done *right*. Just look at the website for Aunt Pat's that you've put up online . . . you've single-handedly moved this restaurant into the twenty-first century!"

Derrick looked doubtful, but at least Lulu got a smile from him. "Thanks, Granny Lulu. Sometimes, you know, you just don't feel like you're doing anything right. But I like Peaches a lot. I just hope she sticks around long enough to catch me doing something I can be proud of."

Lulu looked sadly after him as he walked out of the office to get a snack from the kitchen. Derrick still felt like he had to earn everyone's approval. She cursed his mother for the hundredth time for doing that to him.

The scene with Derrick had made her feel down. A surefire way to cheer herself up was to visit with her guests in the restaurant dining room. On any given day, half the people in the room were regulars she could greet by name. And the dining room itself, with its old brick walls, dark wooden booths, and creaky hardwood floors was comforting in itself—it took her back to a simpler time when Aunt Pat was the one laughing and cutting up with her guests.

Sure enough, as soon as she walked into the dining room, she started smiling. Some of her favorite people were sitting there together. The Graces and the Back Porch Blues Band were all sitting at a corner booth with a table pulled next to it. They all called out a greeting to her as she walked up.

"Where's Flo?" she asked. "Didn't y'all invite her to join in?"

Evelyn said coolly, "Working on the wedding from hell, of course. I firmly believe that union is cursed from the very start."

Lulu said mildly, "Oh, I wouldn't go that far, Evelyn. You know, weddings are stressful times for everybody. That little girl is probably a lot easier to deal with ordinarily than she is now."

"Well, she sure is more like Bridezilla than Cinderella. And her mother really is a piece of work."

Buddy said, "At least we've all got a little work from it, though. I even had the Back Porch Blues Band some business cards made up, in case anybody at the wedding wants us to play a gig for them."

Peggy Sue chirped up, "Now that's something I need to be doing, Buddy. Maybe I can get some cards made up for our flower-arranging business."

"Here comes the lady of the hour now," said Evelyn in a dry voice as Flo fluttered up.

"Who've we got here?" she said without even saying hi. She started counting heads. "Peggy Sue, Evelyn, Buddy . . . *Good!* Group meeting! Group meeting!"

Evelyn made a face. "Aren't you getting kind of wound up about this wedding business? Anyone would think that *you* were the one getting hitched."

"God forbid!" said Flo. "It's bad enough dealing with someone else's nonsense. I'm just trying to get this wedding set up so that these people are happy and we all end up looking good, that's all."

Morty said, "It should be a slam dunk, Flo. You've got the best help in town. We'll rock the reception with our tunes, the flowers will beautify the room, and you've got the best barbeque in Memphis for the guests to enjoy for the reception."

Big Ben bellowed, "And the reception is at Graceland in the car museum. So you got all Elvis's toys in the room for decoration. Man, those guests are going to be in hog heaven."

Flo waved her hand impatiently. "I know all that, y'all. But I'm still trying to make sure that everything goes *perfectly*. Even if you have the absolute *best* people, in the absolute *best* venue, things can still go wrong unless you organize so everybody knows what everybody else is doing."

Evelyn said, "Honey, it's self-evident. Peggy Sue, Jeanne, and I are helping with the flowers. Ben and Oliver and Lulu are doing food. Sara's going to hold things down at Aunt Pat's while we're at Graceland. Buddy, Morty, and Big Ben are in charge of the music. Cherry is the general dogsbody. Easy-peasy."

Cherry said, "General *dogsbody*? Can't I be something else?"

"You'll be indispensible when Flo needs an extra set of hands," said Lulu soothingly.

"I was thinking," said Morty in a mulling-over voice, "that I would get a small token of appreciation for the bride and her mother. For giving us the gig, you know. Do you know the kinds of thing they like, Flo?"

Flo was used to trains of thought that got derailed by

this group. "I don't know them very well personally, but I know that the stores the bride is registered with are listed on her website. And Cynthia—the bride's mother? She's even got a link on the bride's site—you know, for the guests who want to give her a hostess gift and things like that."

There was a heavy silence. "You mean to tell me," said Big Ben in his loud voice, "that this young lady is *telling* people what she wants them to give her? And her mother is, too?"

Flo explained patiently, "She's not *making* people give her certain things, Big Ben. Just making it easier for people who want to give her something in her china pattern. She also mentions that she accepts cash or checks if someone doesn't want to mess with the registry sites."

More stunned silence.

"Now you all know that times have changed! Y'all should be well aware of all that," said Flo, putting her hands on her hips.

Peggy Sue said, "I knew times had changed, but I didn't think *people* had. Does the bride carry around a credit card machine in case a guest wants to whip out their card?"

Flo sighed. "No, there's nothing crazy like that going on."

Lulu said, "I wonder if the groom has a website and what *he's* asking for?"

Cherry covered her ears with manicured hands. "La, la, la! It's too much! It's boggling my mind!"

"The groom has a very nice, very discreet little website," said Flo. "He's looking for donations for the honeymoon and the rehearsal dinner."

There was a collective groan from the group.

Flo said, "But never mind all that, y'all! If you *want* to make a little gift, I'm sure they'd be happy with any little thank-you . . . like a tin of nuts or a fruit basket, or something like that." But she sounded less than sure.

"Anyway," Flo continued brightly, "I'm going to send everybody a joint e-mail about times to arrive at the wedding and the schedule for setting equipment up and all of that." She sent around a piece of paper to get everyone's e-mail address. "Because things *do* go wrong *all* the time. Some of it we can help, and then I'll feel better about the stuff we *can't* help—like the way my photographer is sick."

Evelyn said, "Holden isn't feeling well?"

"No. Well, I guess he's *feeling* well, but he's not sounding well. His voice is like . . . gone. Just a weird squeak is all. He warbled out something about having laryngitis when I called this morning to check in with him."

Lulu frowned. "That doesn't really matter, does it? Does he really need his voice?"

"But if you think about it, the photographer *does* need to talk. He needs to call out for everybody to watch the cake get cut or tell the mom's side of the family that they're going to be the focus for the next picture. You know. The photographer is kind of a director." Flo looked seriously peeved.

"Tell you what," said Peggy Sue eagerly. "If I see

some movement toward the wedding cake, I'll holler at everybody. I'm all *about* the cake, honey."

"I'm all about the cake if it's *good* cake. Some of those wedding cakes look really pretty, but they taste just like cardboard," said Lulu with a face.

"This will be *delicious* cake. That's because Tommie said she'd make it for us when the baker backed out," said Flo.

"They upset the baker, too?" demanded Cherry.

"These people seem to have a God-given talent for making folks upset," said Flo with a shrug of her shoulders. "Who am I to argue with a gift?"

Chapter

17

Flo said, between her teeth, "It's going to be *perfect*. A *beautiful* wedding."

"It's hardly even enough rain to dampen your hair," said Lulu in a soothing tone. "And the temperature will drop a little with these clouds and things will just *feel* so much better." Which was, of course, a total lie. Rain in the Southern heat meant humidity—not cooler temperatures.

Flo appreciated the lie and smiled at Lulu. "Thanks. I've just got to calm down and not get all wound up about stuff I don't have any control over."

The bride's mother, Cynthia, marched up to Flo. It was clear she was *not* going to try to calm down. "They're all coming! All of them!"

Flo put a well-manicured hand to her throat. "The guests? They're *all* coming? They *can't* all be coming!

Almost half of them didn't even RSVP and then there were about thirty of them that said for sure that they weren't going to be here at all."

"Well, maybe," said Cynthia in a sarcastic voice, "I'm just imagining things, but it sure does look like my friends and relatives out there, coming in on the shuttles."

"But we're not going to have enough food! Or seats at the reception! And the chapel only seats seventy-five. . . . Any more than that and it'll be standing-room only."

"I'm not paying you good money for *me* to worry about this," said Cynthia with hard eyes. "You just make sure it all works out. I want this wedding *perfect*." She stalked off.

"Okay," said Lulu, "Calm down, Flo. We'll make the best of this, honey. Why don't you take care of the chapel seating, since that comes first. Ask the Graceland coordinator for folding chairs. It'll work out—I'm sure these folks are going to see what's happened and will let the older guests sit down. And so what if there are people standing in the back? The ceremony will only be twenty-five minutes, tops."

"What about the food?" asked Flo nervously.

"Just leave that up to Ben and Oliver. We'll call Derrick and have him bring some more food from the restaurant. We have this sort of thing happen all the time, Flo—in the restaurant business you never really know how many people you'll have to feed that day. Sometimes we get swamped, too."

For a while, "making do" went pretty well. Flo felt calmer about her last-minute emergency—until she spilled a large container of sweet tea on the front of her dress. She cursed and said, "What the heck am I going to do now? I can't go to the ceremony like this!"

It did look like Flo had had some sort of restroom accident, thought Lulu. Cherry jumped in with a rescue line. "Come on, Flo—you can borrow my dress. We'll trade out in the restroom and I'll hang out in there for a while and dry yours with the hand dryer."

Flo was beyond caring that Cherry had on a banana yellow dress with a large print of hot peppers covering it. "Bless you, Cherry! I just need something dry." A few minutes later, Flo was back out, dashing around with her clipboard and Cherry was standing in the restroom in her slip drying Flo's dress under the hand dryers.

Lulu called Derrick's cell phone. "Hon? Could you run into the kitchen and see how much food we've got already prepared or what can be cooked up real quick?" She waited for a minute while Derrick rattled off a list of the available foods. "What? Okay, that'll have to do. Can you bring most of that pork over and all the sides? We've got more guests than we bargained for. If I have to shortchange everybody on the barbeque a little, I can make up for it with more sides. Oh, and however much tea you can bring over, too." She stopped. "You know, that's going to be too much stuff for you to handle. Why don't you call Peaches over to help you bring it by?"

Derrick said reluctantly, "I'm not so sure. She might be in the middle of doing something else, since it's Saturday." He paused. "Oh. Actually, she just walked into the restaurant, so never mind. I'll see if she can help me out."

Lulu popped into the restroom to see how things were going. Cherry still stood there, holding Flo's dress under the dryer. "It's coming along," she said. "But it's slow."

Peggy Sue and Evelyn both hurried into the room. "At least our part is all done! The flowers are all set and they look *beautiful*, y'all!" said Peggy Sue, beaming as she rummaged in her pocketbook for a lipstick.

"What are you doing about the extra tables that we need for the reception?" asked Lulu.

Evelyn waved her hand dismissively. "Well, you can't whip up extra flowers just thirty minutes before the reception starts. We put some magnolia blossoms and greenery on the table and they looked just fine."

Peggy Sue gave a nervous giggle. "It's been kind of a disaster so far, hasn't it? What kind of people don't RSVP to a wedding and then show up? Don't they know that'll mess everybody up?"

"And I *expected* the batty bride, crazy mother, and silent groom to be weird, but what's eating Oliver today?" asked Evelyn. "He's acting really odd himself. He's white as a sheet, keeps looking over his shoulder, and then on top of it all, his mind has clearly been somewhere else."

"Maybe it's the guilt eating him alive," intoned Peggy Sue. "Maybe he's the killer! And he's on the lookout for his next victim. Watch out, Graceland!"

"Or maybe," said Lulu in a dry voice, "he's just not

feeling well. God forbid that's the case, because I can't really afford to lose any kitchen help today. Maybe I should go out and check on him." She had turned to go out the restroom door when the door opened abruptly in her face, making her scoot back a couple of feet.

Flo was there, hair wild like she'd been running her fingers through it. "Flowers! Flowers for the extra tables! Tablecloths! Ohmigod, tablecloths!"

Evelyn said, "Honey, it's all been handled."

"What? How . . ."

"It's been handled. It looks good! Just go and worry about something else, okay? Oh . . . and do something about your hair. It looks like the Bride of Frankenstein."

Flo pushed past Cherry to the mirror. She put down a pile of notebooks on the counter and ran her hands through her hair. "Better?" she asked Evelyn.

Evelyn just stared at her. "Better if you're trying to look worse."

Peggy Sue said, "For heaven's sake, Flo! Stand still a second." And Peggy Sue pulled a loaded cosmetic bag out of her enormous pocketbook. She took out a brush and expertly whipped Flo's hair into a semblance of its normal self. "And you can use some color, too—you look like hell, honey." She squinted at Flo's dress and shook her head. "Here's my red lipstick. . . . Try it on."

Flo leaned into the mirror and ran the lipstick over her mouth. "Got to *go*," she said, dashing back out the door.

"That's my signal, too." Lulu sighed. "I'd better go across the street and make sure that meat and those sides got here. And that Oliver isn't off being sick somewhere, I guess. Evelyn, can you give me a hand? I'm thinking we could go ahead and fill some tea glasses while the ceremony is going on."

"I'll come help, too, as soon as this dress looks presentable," said Cherry, nodding at the still sopping party dress.

Derrick and Peaches were just unloading the last of the food when Lulu walked up to them. Ben stood there with arms crossed. "These folks are going to have to wait a little while until the extra food is cooked. That's the problem with not getting an accurate head count."

The Graceland wedding coordinator who'd been checking in with Ben said, "I don't think you'll have to worry about it. We've got the bar set up over here and this crowd looks like they'll be happy to visit and have a couple of drinks for a little while. And they're right here in the car museum, so they can walk around and look at Elvis's pink Cadillac or his motorcycles . . . or the pink Jeep. There's going to be plenty for them to do." She looked at her watch. "I'd better head over to the ceremony." She looked across the road at Graceland and stared. "Is that a woman in a slip running across the front yard?"

Evelyn drawled, "Clarice, you should be able to recognize that red hair. It's your very own docent, Cherry Hayes, tearing across Graceland in her petticoats."

"But what is she . . . "

"It never pays to ask, Clarice. Better get crackin'—I think that ceremony is about to start up in the chapel."

Evelyn, Peggy Sue, and Peaches were already busily tackling the table settings. Ben was cooking at a frantic pace. "Ben, honey, where is Oliver? He needs to be helping you out."

Ben shrugged, his back to her as he worked. "Mother, I don't really know. He was here just a little while ago, although he looked really sick. Said he had to go take care of something real quick. You mind finding him for me? I could use the extra hands."

Lulu was on her way out to find Oliver when she felt a tap on her shoulder and turned to see Derrick behind her. "What should I be doing, Granny Lulu?"

Lulu looked around. "Where's Peaches?"

Derrick shrugged. "She's helping out the Graces with the tables. But that stuff looks like it's all under control."

Lulu thought about it. "Either help your Uncle Ben out in the kitchen or maybe help Big Ben, Morty, and Buddy set up the electrical system and speakers? Just hop in." She saw that Derrick wasn't completely comfortable with either of those assignments. "Or you could ask Ben what to do if you're not sure how to prepare the food, you know. Just ask him."

"I hate to interrupt him when he's tearing around trying to throw this stuff together," said Derrick in a low voice.

"Or hunt me down and ask me, sweetie, if you have any questions about cooking the food. I can give you whatever directions you need. Just find me," said Lulu. "And now I'm sorry, Derrick, but I've got to run, hon."

She absently patted him on the arm and jogged off to find Oliver.

It didn't take her long to find him. He was outside the car museum around a corner, talking very quietly to Holden Parsons.

"Holden! Honey, you need to run over to the chapel—they're getting ready to start the ceremony!"

Holden looked startled. He opened his mouth to say something, but whatever he was trying to say came out in an odd squeaking whisper. He started running toward the street to cross over to the wedding chapel.

"I don't believe it!" said Lulu, gaping at the road. "Look! There's some guests that are parking right there on the side of the road in Elvis's *yard*. Well, the fence is there, but nobody is supposed to be parking right there on Elvis Presley Boulevard. I hope somebody gets them to move their cars before the cops get here." She looked at Oliver, who seemed like he was a million miles away. "Aren't you feeling well, hon? I hate to say it, but you really need to be over there giving Ben a hand. He's got all this extra food to fix now, since all those guests showed up." She peered closer at Oliver.

"There's just something eating me up right now, Lulu. All I keep thinking about is how I don't want to go to jail. I don't. I'd die in there—there's no way I could survive in that place."

Lulu thought about what Tudy had said about how devastated Oliver had been at the failure of his restaurant. And what Derrick had told her about how Oliver had been furious about Adam and bashed him on the Internet. And what Big Jack had said about Oliver pushing Adam down the stairs in the parking deck. And that he'd argued with Ginger the day she died. Lulu gave a shiver even though the day was hot. No one could see her right here, around the corner of the museum.

But it still just didn't seem to fit. "Oliver, what are you talking about? I don't think you killed Adam. I know you were furious with him, but from what I understand, he got up and walked away after you pushed him."

Oliver looked startled. "How did you know about that?"

"Big Jack told me. He only told me because he knew I could keep a secret. You were kind of worrying me a second ago, getting so serious. But I'm right, aren't I? You were so scared and horrified at the thought that you'd killed Adam that you weren't about to try to kill him again. Besides, you already thought he was dead."

Oliver hung his head. "Big Jack told me not to tell a soul about it. I guess because I involved him in it when I thought I'd murdered Adam. I *was* horrified. But who knows—I might have tried to kill him again if I'd known he was still alive. Especially since he would have told the police what I'd done and I'd have been arrested for assault."

"And Ginger? You *were* talking to her that day that Jeanne saw you, weren't you? I'm guessing you didn't want to admit it because she was blackmailing you— Pink told me that Ginger and Adam had a little black-mailing business going and Ginger must have inherited it when Adam died."

"She was *trying* to blackmail me," said Oliver, looking blankly across at the wall.

"What I don't understand is what Ginger knew. Did Adam have something on you before he died? But I thought you didn't even know who he really was."

"I didn't. No, Ginger thought up her very own angle this time—Adam had talked to her on the phone right after he pulled himself off the bottom of the staircase. So she thought the police might want to know that I'd already tried to kill Adam once that day."

Lulu said, "And you didn't take the bait?"

"No. I was tired of the whole thing by then. I figured that even if I started paying her to keep quiet that somehow the police might figure out what had happened. They'd already found the stuff I'd written online and figured out that I fit the description of the guy having the argument with Adam in the restaurant. And I *didn't* kill Adam. It didn't really matter if Ginger said anything or not."

Lulu glanced at her watch and winced. But she still needed to know. "Did you kill Ginger? Did you decide to just shut her up permanently so you wouldn't have to keep paying her?"

"No. I didn't."

"Oliver, where were you the afternoon Ginger was killed?" Oliver opened his mouth up quickly, and Lulu held up her hand to stop him. "And I know it wasn't at the dentist office because Tudy told me y'all had to pay a missed-appointment fee. And—where was Tudy? She said she was at home, upset about you, but Evelyn saw her driving around that afternoon."

Oliver swallowed hard. "No, I wasn't at the doctor. I forgot all about that appointment after Ginger and I had that argument. I just went out to the park and hung out there for a while, thinking about the mess I was in."

"Well, honey, you don't even know the half of the mess you're in. Tudy thinks you were cheating on her with Ginger. She was with Jeanne that afternoon and saw you with Ginger. And she knew you were sneaking around and hiding things from her, but she didn't know what. She thought you were being sneaky because you were having an affair."

Oliver rubbed his very large forehead like it was hurting him badly.

Lulu asked quietly, "Do you think Tudy had anything to do with Ginger's death? She was awfully mad at the thought Ginger had stolen you away from her."

Oliver shook his head. "Lulu! You know Tudy wouldn't do something like that. She was probably just driving around that afternoon looking for *me*. That's all." But his eyes didn't look as convinced as his voice.

"Look, Lulu," he said, "it's been good talking to you, but I've got to help Ben out with that food."

Lulu still wondered what Holden had been talking to Oliver about so intently. But Oliver was already dashing inside the car museum to help Ben. She couldn't see him killing Adam—not after thinking he was already dead before. But Ginger? He'd sure looked upset at the idea of going to prison . . . and getting rid of Ginger would be a little bit of insurance that the police wouldn't find out about his fight with Adam.

She jumped as her cell phone starting singing "Zip-a-Dee-Doo-Dah." "Hello?"

"Where in the hell is Holden?" squeaked Flo in a hoarse voice.

"Up at the ceremony! I just sent him packing up there ten minutes ago with his camera in his hand. And he was running, too. He's *got* to be over there."

Flo gave a sob. "But he's not! And Cynthia is on the warpath. The guests are all crammed into the chapel because there's too many of them and I don't even have all of the bridal party together!"

"Flo, it's going to be *perfect*," said Lulu, picking up Flo's mantra. "I'm going to find Holden. And if I can't, I'll take pictures with the digital camera I brought—it's better than nothing. You just calm down your mother of the bride and round up the wedding party." And she charged across the street to the chapel.

Lulu tried to think, which was hard to do when her head was pounding. Where could Holden be? The chapel was in the woods next to the mansion and clearly he wasn't there with Flo. Could he still be trying to take some pictures around the mansion like he did at the car museum?

She couldn't believe he'd have gone *inside* Graceland right before the ceremony. But could he have been taking pictures around the exterior of the house? And that's when she found him *inside* the wrought iron gate around

Elvis' pool. In a restricted area. "Holden! They need you . . ." She dropped off as she saw the reason he was in there at all—Big Jack was standing behind him, near the bushes on the inside of the fence. Holden's camera was at the bottom of the swimming pool. And Big Jack looked to be holding a gun pointed directly at Holden.

Chapter

18

"Great," snarled Big Jack. "Holden, you have Lulu Taylor to thank for what I'm about to do. I *was* just going to make sure you understood how serious I was and let you go. But now that Lulu's here, I'll need to get rid of both of you and give myself a head start to get out of town."

Lulu said in a hoarse voice, "Holden took a picture of you with Ginger, didn't he? So you threw his camera in the pool."

"Of course. It's a digital camera. And I was just having a friendly little talk with him a minute ago, making sure he hadn't uploaded those pictures onto a computer or a phone or anything. And then we were just going to go our own ways with the understanding that he was never going to say a word about that picture and that it was never going to surface anywhere . . . or he'd be very sorry. But that plan is all shot to hell now."

Holden was ashen and looked at Lulu in desperation. Lulu said, sounding braver than she felt, "Big Jack, you're not going to be able to get away with this. They're already out looking for you—I came out here because Flo said you weren't there," lied Lulu. "You're not going to get that head start you're looking for."

"I think you're wrong," said Big Jack. He cocked the gun at them.

"Where did things start going wrong, Big Jack?" asked Lulu desperately. "You weren't too upset when Adam died. You must have been the one to kill him, though. Because that's why Holden has a photo of you with Ginger from the day she died, right? She was blackmailing you over murdering Adam."

"Among other things," said Big Jack dryly. "She picked up where Adam left off—they were like blackmailing business partners or something. So she had me over a barrel with the affair—and she knew I was on the scene at Adam's murder."

"Because she was there, too, wasn't she? Ginger had been talking on the phone to Adam right before his death—that's why she knew Oliver had pushed him down the stairs. And when she caught up with Adam, you were already there, arguing with him. And you had a gun."

"I wasn't even going to *do* anything with that gun!" said Big Jack, holding out one hand beseechingly. "I just wanted to scare some sense into Adam and let him know that I was not going to be blackmailed for the rest of my life. Something was going to have to change."

Lulu said thoughtfully, "One thing about Ginger that week . . . she was really fired up. She had this huge argument with Evelyn in Aunt Pat's. She had a fight with Adam and dumped him—at least for a little while. I bet she was still really fired up at that point. Did she take your gun and shoot him with it? Since you weren't going to shoot him."

Big Jack gave a short laugh. "The crazy woman. Yeah, she said, 'Give me that gun. You know you aren't supposed to point a gun at somebody unless you plan on using it.' I was surprised to see her there and just handed the thing over. And then she shot him right in the chest. I couldn't believe it. Kept thinking the cops would be over in a flash, but there was all this construction noise going on and nobody seemed to notice."

"And nobody even saw you."

"That was weird, too! It was like I was meant to get away with it. There we were, right by the river in front of a condo. But we were kind of in the trees—I didn't want anybody to see me arguing with Adam so I'd dragged him over there to talk to him on the sly."

"So there you were with a dead body, shot with *your* gun, and a woman who had proof you'd been blackmailed by the victim."

Big Jack nodded and pointed the gun more directly at Lulu. Lulu said quickly, "And Holden took pictures the day Ginger died—but he only mentioned seeing Oliver in them. But I'm thinking he must have gotten a picture of you, too, since his camera is at the bottom of the pool."

Big Jack drawled, "Oh he got a picture of me. . . .

He just didn't realize he had until yesterday. He took a closer look at the photo of Ginger and Oliver and saw me, sitting in my car, watching them. I was tailing Ginger to get her alone."

Lulu swallowed. "When we were at the lake house, I asked Holden to send me those pictures. You must have realized what I'd find if I studied them closely. So you called me the night I got home from the lake. You must have had some device to disguise your voice. You warned me off the case so I wouldn't remind Holden about the pictures.

"Not that warning you did a lick of good." Big Jack motioned for Lulu to move closer to Holden. "Chat time's over."

Lulu scrambled to delay him. "And I didn't realize it until just now, but you messed up when you told me about Evelyn pointing her little gun at Ginger. When we were at the funeral, the very day you murdered Ginger, you said you were driving directly out of town to go see your accountant. So you *shouldn't* have been in Memphis to see Evelyn do anything at all!"

Big Jack drawled, "Aren't you such a clever one. That's right. . . . I was weaving a tangled web for myself, wasn't I?" He pointed the gun at Lulu.

They were standing right next to the pool. Lulu searched her brain for something, anything at all, to stop him. "They're going to hear the gunshots, Big Jack!"

"Yeah, but by the time they figure out where they came from, I'll be out of here. It'll take them a while to find you in the pool."

Lulu looked behind Big Jack and her eyes widened until she quickly trained them back on Big Jack. Derrick was stealthily climbing over the wrought iron fence. Then he started running at Big Jack before slipping on the slick brick surrounding the pool. Derrick careened into Big Jack, knocking them both in the water along with the gun . . . and Holden. Who couldn't swim.

Holden grasped frantically at Derrick while Big Jack pulled himself out of the pool and took off at a run. Lulu looked around for something to hand to Derrick to pull him and Holden to safety—but all she saw were planters and benches.

That's when Cherry, who was wearing Flo's dress that she'd *finally* gotten dry, dashed up, dove into the pool, and put Holden's neck in the crook of her arm to pull him to the side.

Derrick by now was climbing out of the pool and coughing a little before jogging off in the direction that Big Jack had gone in. Lulu took off after him at a much slower pace.

In the most perfect timing ever, the Memphis police had discovered the cars parked on both sides of Elvis Pressley Boulevard, right in front of the mansion. The cars were blocking the lanes and the police were determined to find the perpetrators, give them a ticket, and make them park in the main parking lot—and take the shuttle to Graceland like everybody else. They pulled up to the gate of the mansion and strode down the driveway.

Where they encountered a sopping wet Big Jack tearing across the lawn followed by an equally wet and out of breath teenage boy and an older lady yelling for help. They weren't sure exactly what was going on, but they were happy to detain the man everyone was chasing after to find out.

"Okay, so it wasn't a *perfect* wedding," said Flo after all the guests and the wedding party had left. She was about halfway through a leftover bottle of chardonnay. "The man who was giving away the bride was arrested for murder. The photographer's camera was destroyed. And Lulu and Holden were nearly murdered during the ceremony. But it was as perfect as it *could* be."

"Amen to that," sighed Lulu, carefully propping her now aching feet up on a chair across from her.

"And Cherry helped save the day," said Flo, raising her wineglass to her. "Considering I'd left the groom's ring in that darned restroom."

Cherry grinned and Lulu said, "There aren't many friends who'd run across Graceland in their slip to make sure the groom's ring was at the chapel before the ceremony started."

"Not having the ring would have been a disaster," agreed Flo. "Although not quite as bad as two dead bodies in the Graceland swimming pool."

"I just can't believe that Big Jack was the murderer," said Evelyn, coming back inside the car museum. She'd gone outside for a smoke and seemed well on her way to getting hooked again.

Lulu said, "Well, he was and he wasn't. He didn't actually kill Adam, you know. He threatened him with a gun, but he didn't *kill* him."

"No," said Evelyn in a dejected tone, "that would be my friend Ginger."

"Well, she was awfully mad at Adam," said Cherry. Lulu was proud that Cherry was managing to keep an "I told you so" tone out of her voice. "And she had a right to be."

"I guess I'm lucky she didn't shoot *me*," said Evelyn gloomily. "But Big Jack did kill Ginger. And he was about to kill Holden and you, too, Lulu."

Flo ran her thin hands through her hair until it poofed out in an even bigger bouffant than usual. "I just don't know how he thought he was going to get away with it all. We totally would have heard those gunshots in the chapel."

"But you wouldn't have known exactly where the sound had come from," said Lulu. "And you wouldn't know who'd done it, either."

"We'd have known Big Jack was missing!" said Flo heatedly, still vexed that the bride had had to have some random third cousin to step in for Big Jack.

"But as far as *you* knew, Big Jack was off being sick in the bathroom or had had car trouble on the way over to Graceland, or something like that. You wouldn't have automatically gone to the police and told them that Big Jack had just shot two people," said Evelyn.

"I think Big Jack felt like killing Ginger was justified," mused Lulu. "Here he was, running for office. And he *hadn't* killed Adam. But here this woman was, trying to blackmail him on two different things. And he knew he couldn't really stop her. It *had* been his gun. And he was the one with the issue with Adam. So he decided the easiest thing would be to get rid of her. And he probably figured that she wasn't all that great of a person anyway. Maybe he even justified it by thinking he'd helped make the world a better place."

"Were you just scared to death?" asked Flo with a shiver. "When he was standing right there in front of you with that gun?"

"It *did* scare me," said Lulu, feeling suddenly very tired. "Because it wasn't the Big Jack I knew standing there. It was somebody else; somebody who would shoot me and Holden in cold blood and not even think twice about it. Thank God for Derrick. He came flying at him right out of the blue."

"And thank God you told him to find you if he had any questions about setting up the food or the band," said Evelyn.

Lulu teared up a little. "And here he's been so insecure the last couple of weeks. His mom really messed him up, you know? He's been feeling like he's not any good. And here he is saving two lives in one fell swoop." She took out a tissue and blew her nose.

Peggy Sue beamed. "I *knew* he was the perfect match for Peaches! She was the first on the scene after the police, you know. She was worried sick about him, but so *proud*! She went and put a tablecloth around him . . . because he was sopping wet, you know. And ever since she's just been praising him for his act of bravery. Kind of chokes you up . . ." And Peggy Sue choked up on cue, patting herself comfortingly on her shoulder.

"And Cherry saved the day *again* when she jumped in the pool and saved Holden from drowning," said Lulu. "'Cause Holden had fallen in on the diving board side of the pool, so that water was deep. And he couldn't swim a lick."

Cherry beamed. "It *was* a good day for me, wasn't it? Well, y'all know I used to be a lifeguard back in the day. Waaaay back in the day. But some things you just never forget. I was more worried about Derrick at first—I thought Holden might accidentally drown him with all that desperate clawing he was doing. But we got it all straightened out."

Ben and Oliver came out of the kitchen where they'd just finished cleaning up. "I missed all the action today, didn't I?" He gave his mother a hug. "This is a wedding that I'll never forget."

"At least the food worked out okay," said Oliver. "Thanks for giving me the gig, buddy."

"I don't know if you should thank me or not," drawled Ben, "considering how dangerous it ended up being."

The Graces were still chattering excitedly about the events of the day when Lulu stepped outside to check on Big Ben, Buddy, and Morty to see if they needed any help taking down the equipment. Oliver followed her outside.

Oliver let go a deep breath. "I'm just glad this is all over. Now I don't have to worry about anybody black-mailing me or trying to ruin my life. I feel like I've got my *life* back. And it makes me that more determined to find a job."

Lulu hesitated. "Oliver, I didn't want to mention this because I worried it might offend you. I mean, the job is totally beneath you. And I know you want to open your own restaurant again. But we've got an open spot for a manager at Aunt Pat's. I've gotten to the point where I just want to sit around and visit with people, Ben's always in the kitchen. Ben's wife, Sara, is too busy with her art and would rather wait tables than worry about the business side of a restaurant. Derrick loves the business end, but he's still in school. . . ." Her voice trailed off.

Oliver's eyes got misty. "Lulu, I love you! Thank you so much." He gave Lulu a big hug.

"And if you find something else or find a business partner to start up a new restaurant, I'll completely understand. But this way at least you'll still be working in a restaurant and making a little money." And not driving Tudy completely crazy at home, thought Lulu. The poor thing.

Oliver and Lulu walked back inside. Flo was saying, "And, y'all, the wedding, despite everything, was a huge success. I had two people ask for my business card. I gave the number for Aunt Pat's to one person, Peggy Sue's number for flower arranging once, and gave the card for the Back Porch Blues Band to two different people after Morty played that wonderful harmonica solo."

Cherry mused, "I think I need to make myself up a business card and offer my services, too. I could be Cherry Hayes, Lifeguard. Or Cherry Hayes, Party Saver."

"And Derrick could get a bodyguard business card," said Peggy Sue. "Maybe he could add it to his resume and end up protecting the president one day." She smiled at the idea of Peaches and Derrick living in wedded bliss in D.C. while protecting the president.

Lulu said, "Well, that's something else if we almost had two murders taking place at the party and folks still want to use us. That's saying something about the food, music, and flowers."

"Well, of *course* it was perfect," said Flo. "Between Graceland and Aunt Pat's barbeque, how could you go wrong?"

Recipes
Put Some South in Your Mouth

Tommie's Peach Cobbler

2 cups fresh ripe peaches
1½ cups of sugar
1 stick of margarine
¾ cup of flour
2 teaspoons baking powder
¼ teaspoon salt
¾ cup milk

Mix peaches and ½ cup sugar; set aside. Preheat oven to 375 degrees Fahrenheit. Melt butter in a 9-inch by 9-inch container. Mix other ingredients into a batter and pour over the melted margarine. (Make sure you don't stir.) Place the peach mixture on top of the batter (still don't stir). The peaches will sink to the bottom. Bake at 375 degrees for 40 minutes or until the crust is lightly browned. Serve warm.

Lulu's Vidalia Onion Dip

5 or 6 Vidalia onions, sliced

¾ cup vinegar

¾ cup sugar

2 cups water

½ cup mayonnaise

1 teaspoon celery seed

Thinly slice the onions and soak them for 2 to 4 hours in the vinegar, sugar, and water. Drain well. Toss onions with mayonnaise and celery seed. Serve on crackers.

◇◇◇◇◇◇◇◇◇

Lulu's Spicy Cheese Straws

1 pound sharp cheese, grated

3 cups flour, sifted

1 cup softened margarine

1 teaspoon salt

½ teaspoon cayenne pepper

Preheat oven to 325 degrees Fahrenheit. Grate cheese. Mix ingredients together. Put dough in a cookie press. Line cookie sheets with parchment paper. Press the dough onto the cookie sheet and cut to desired length. Cook in 325-degree oven for 15 minutes or until brown. Allow to cool.

◇◇◇◇◇◇◇◇◇

Grits Breakfast Casserole

1 cup grits, uncooked

4 cups water

1 stick butter

1 box cornbread mix

8 slices bacon, cooked and crumbled (or substitute 1
     pound cooked sausage if you like a little more pop)

1 cup milk

1 cup cheese, shredded

4 eggs

1 teaspoon salt

Preheat oven to 325 degrees Fahrenheit. Add 1 cup uncooked grits to 4 cups boiling water, 1 teaspoon salt, and 1 stick of butter. Reduce heat, cover, and simmer about 5 minutes, until liquid has been absorbed. Remove from the heat.

Cook bacon, drain, and crumble.

Beat the 4 eggs with 1 cup milk.

Mix everything together with 1 box of cornbread mix. Pour into a 13-inch by 9-inch casserole dish that has been sprayed with cooking spray. Sprinkle the cheese on the top.

Bake at 325 degrees Fahrenheit for 30 minutes.

Brunswick Stew

1 chicken (4-pound fowl)

1 quart corn

1 quart fresh tomatoes, chopped

1 pint okra, chopped

1 pint butter beans

2 onions, chopped

Salt and pepper to taste

Boil chicken until it's tender. Pull meat from bones and cut it into big cubes (don't throw out the broth in the pot). Put the cubes back into the broth. Add vegetables to pot and cook until the liquid thickens and the vegetables are well done. Simmer over low heat for approximately 3 to 4 hours, stirring occasionally.

◇◇◇◇◇◇◇◇◇

Black-Eyed Pea Salad

2 15-ounce cans black-eyed peas, drained

¾ cup red onion, chopped

¾ cup green pepper, chopped

1 teaspoon garlic powder

¼ cup vinegar

¼ cup sugar

2 tablespoons olive oil

Hot sauce and ground black pepper to taste

Combine the first 4 ingredients. Combine remaining ingredients and pour over the pea mixture. Season with hot sauce and ground black pepper to taste. Refrigerate for 12 hours or more.

◇◇◇◇◇◇◇◇◇

Southern Spiced Tea

16 cups water

5 tablespoons tea leaves

Juice of 6 oranges

Juice of 1 lemon

2 cups sugar

1 teaspoon whole cloves

Add the tea leaves to 8 cups boiling water. Let stand 5 minutes, then strain. Make a syrup by boiling the sugar, cloves, and 8 cups of water together. Add the syrup and the fruit juices to the tea. (This makes about 18 cups.)

Mix thoroughly. Serve over ice.

◇◇◇◇◇◇◇◇◇

New South–Style Peach Glaze
for Shrimp

½ cup brown sugar

3 tablespoons cold water

2 cups peaches, diced and peeled

4 tablespoons bourbon

3 tablespoons green onions, minced

½ teaspoon ground ginger

¼ teaspoon ground cinnamon

Salt and pepper to taste

In a cast-iron or heavy saucepan, stir brown sugar over medium heat until caramelized.

Add 3 tablespoons of cold water. Add the remaining ingredients to pan and cook until the mixture is syrupy (about 10 to 15 minutes). Remove from heat. Pour the mixture into a blender and puree until smooth. Salt and pepper to taste.

◇◇◇◇◇◇◇◇◇

Tommie's Pecan Pie

3 eggs, slightly beaten

1 cup Karo syrup

1 cup sugar

²/₃ cup pecans, chopped

1 teaspoon vanilla

¹/₈ teaspoon salt

2 tablespoons butter, melted

9-inch unbaked pie shell

Preheat oven to 450 degrees Fahrenheit. Mix together all of the ingredients. Pour into the pie shell. Bake at 450 degrees for 10 minutes. Reduce the heat to 350 degrees and bake for 30 to 35 minutes or until a blade inserted in the center comes out clean.

NEW FROM ANTHONY AND BARRY AWARD WINNER

JULIE HYZY

GRACE UNDER PRESSURE

Everyone wants a piece of millionaire Bennett Marshfield, owner of Marshfield Manor, but now it's up to the new curator, Grace Wheaton, and handsome groundskeeper Jack Embers to protect their dear old Marshfield. But to do this, they'll have to investigate a botched Ponzi scheme, some torrid Wheaton family secrets—and sour grapes out for revenge.

penguin.com

TOWN IN A
Blueberry Jam

B. B. HAYWOOD

In the seaside village of Cape Willington, Maine, Candy Holliday has an idyllic life tending to the Blueberry Acres farm she runs with her father. But when an aging playboy and the newly crowned Blueberry Queen are killed, Candy investigates to clear the name of a local handyman. And as she sorts through the town's juicy secrets, things start to get sticky indeed . . .

penguin.com

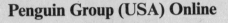